Family Secrets
An Olivia Darrow Mystery, Book 1
S.L. Waters

Published by AB Books, 2020

Table of Contents

One

A harsh beeping reverberates from the void inside my dreams. I grumble as I try to ignore it, but the noise only becomes louder. As I pull my head out from under the covers, I glance over at the cell phone resting on my bedside table. The name flashing across the tiny, clear display causes my heart to drop, and I quickly cover up the lump of flesh beside me. I touch the screen, selecting the video feature while tucking the sheets around my naked body.

"Took you long enough," Frank hisses, his ruddy face coming into view.

"I was sleeping."

"Yeah, right," he snickers. "You're up in the rotation."

"Terrific. What time is it?"

"Just after two in the morning."

"Where am I going?" I grouse.

"Fifth and Lange in your home sector."

"Fuck. Who's the officer on sight?"

"Your favorite, Liv. Growsky," Frank replies, smiling, which grates on my nerves.

"God damn it. Tell him I'll be there in thirty."

I shut off the phone, tossing it onto the floor before turning over and smacking Dean on his firm ass.

"I need you to get up." I try to shove his bulky body, which is nothing but solid muscle. "I gotta go, which means you have to leave."

"Can't Frank get someone else to take the call?"

"I'm next in rotation, so no."

"I think he just wanted to make sure you were alone." Dean lays on top of me, pinning me to the bed. "He needs to get his own fuck buddy. You're mine." His legs spread mine apart, then he penetrates me, and I automatically arch my back.

"You suck," I moan as he fucks me hard. "I need to get going."

"No, you need to get coming."

He flips me over, forces me on my knees, wraps one arm around my waist while using the other to brace himself against the headboard. I have to place my hands on the headboard as well so he doesn't ram me into it when he slams himself inside.

"Fuck, Dean!" I holler.

He rests his head on my sweat-soaked back, driving me hard with each push. My thighs become wet and I scream as I come, drenching my sheets when he pulls out.

"That's better," he says, biting my ass. "I'll see you later, Liv."

The mattress shakes as he gets up while I collapse on the bed in exhaustion. Out of the corner of my eye I catch him smirking as he dresses, his gaze lingering on me. From my angle, he looks taller than his normal six-foot-four. His muscles glisten, enhancing the sheen of the broken arrow tattoo on his left bicep, along with the skull with an intwined snake on his right thigh. His short, dark hair is wet from our activities. He's an officer at station four in Vale and a subordinate to me professionally, so if Frank ever catches us together I'll be demoted. But Dean's great in bed, so to me it's worth the risk. As soon as I hear the front door to my house close, I limp out of bed, my legs shaking.

"Damn it, Dean," I mumble. "One day you're going to break me."

I make my way into the bathroom to take a quick shower before going into my walk-in closet, which is attached to the bathroom. I dress in dark, tight-fitting pants, black boots, and a navy-colored shirt. After running a comb through my straight, dark blond hair, I put it up into a ponytail and grab my holstered gun and credentials off my dresser as well as my cell phone from the floor. I go into the kitchen to eat a protein bar and snatch a container of water while securing my gun to my waist and slipping both my credentials and phone into my back pocket. As I glance out the window above the sink, I notice rain pouring outside, causing the water in my inground pool to overflow.

"Shit."

Because of the weather I'm going to have to take my car instead of the motorcycle I prefer to drive. I pass through the living room, but before I open the door into the garage I grab my black leather jacket from the closet the washer and dryer sit in, step into the garage, and take the keys for the Nimbus. I hit the button to open the hangar-like door on my left as there's another one on the right of the lengthy room where my motorcycle sits.

The Nimbus is the latest sports car to be produced, and they're not cheap. The doors swing up, not out. The body is black with lighted blue neon cords accentuating every curve. It's streamlined to where the front of the car comes almost to a point while the rear sits a little higher. The tires are thick, heavy rubber that grip the road with ease. The interior is a soft, dark material with small blue and silver flecks. I get inside, drop the keys into their holder in the center console, and as I close the door the onboard navigation turns on, illuminating the entire dashboard, which is one flat panel. I touch the screen to get the exact address, which Frank sent to me through my CSB link. The steering wheel extends outward as my seat adjusts to cradle my athletic body, then I step on the gas, the headlights automatically coming on when the car's sensors detect the darkness, the garage door closing behind me as I activate my house alarm from the dashboard.

I work a second job to afford my toys, not unlike many in my profession. The only problem is the type of work I do. I'm a homicide detective for the state of Asmor and a bartender, sometimes waitress, at a strip club called Verdigris. There are only twelve detectives in my division where the others have roughly double that amount, so we're generally overloaded with cases and receive shitty pay for our efforts. Since I'm an unattached woman in her late twenties, I prefer to live in a more upscale sector than where a lot of singles my age or even younger reside. My home sector is known as Range, but it's not a wealthy community by any means. That's reserved solely for those who reside on the island of Waterside, which is seven miles off the coast. It's extremely secluded to the point where you need clearance to even get past the guard station on the mainland before traveling across the bridge or elevated rail that'll take you there.

The other sector most people live in is Berrin, which everyone refers to as the slums. I grew up there after my mother died. My father is still there, but the moment I had enough money I moved back to Range where I'm originally from. To maintain my freedom from the grip the slums have on people, I work two jobs. I make more at the club than I do as a detective, especially with the additional side work I handle for my boss at Verdigris—who's not Frank.

Most of the streets are deserted as I make my way to the north end of the sector. The area isn't hard to find given the heavy police presence in the parking lot of a closed convenience store. As I pull up my headlights flash onto Officer Growsky, who's standing by his vehicle, his one hand resting on the grip of his gun while the other holds an umbrella over his ego-inflated head. My skin crawls at the sight of his balding scalp, worm-like brown mustache, and overweight body, which his uniform can barely contain. He smirks at me while I wait a few extra seconds inside of my nice, dry car before getting drenched.

"Corro said it would be you," Growsky says the second I emerge, referring to Frank by his last name. "Nice wheels, Darrow. How many cocks did you have to suck to buy it?"

It's not a secret to anyone at CSB, whether they're in the headquarters or one of the stations, where I work when I'm not on duty, but Growsky is the only one who brings it up as often, and publicly, as possible. There are many other officers and detectives who work the various venues in Nok for extra cash. For some reason, Growsky has a stick up his ass about where I earn my additional savings.

"Not as many as your wife," I counter, making my way over to the body where several other officers are patiently waiting. "We're having a competition, Glen, and believe it or not she's winning."

He fumes at my comment while everyone else chuckles.

I move beside the white sheet draped over my victim, then roll it back to get a look. Her face is young, her fully exposed body overly thin, but it's clear her breasts have been augmented given their size and the fact they're pointing up instead of having slipped down along her sides like natural ones tend to do when lying on your back. Her hair is short and dyed a bright shade of blue. I notice piercings in her navel and both tits. There's a tattoo of a raven on her right bicep, and a rose along her left hip. The slash across her throat is wide and deep, exposing her trachea. She's lying spread eagle on the rough pavement, her arms pinned against her sides.

"The victim's name is Lesley Marsh," Growsky says, finally joining us. I stand, so he can hand me the scanner he used on the chip embedded just under the skin in her right wrist. "She's nineteen, lives in Berrin, and works at Club Deviant in Nok."

"Who reported her?"

"A passing motorist," he answers. "Guy didn't stick around for us."

"Did you take photos?"

"Already sent them to CSB," he replies, taking his scanner back.

"She's awfully far from home. I wonder what made her come way out here," one of the officers comments, adjusting the sheet so it's back over her body.

"It's more likely a who, not a what," I correct him. "When Lloyd gets here tell him I went to headquarters to get started."

"Sure," Growsky grumbles.

I get back in my car and pull away just as the evidence technicians arrive in their van. After turning left onto Lange, I cross into the Hunnat sector where the entire Civic Security Bureau's network of buildings is housed. All other government agencies, excluding the courthouse, are located in Vale. Hunnat sits in the center of the state just as CSB's headquarters stands erect in the center of the sector. It's thirty-seven stories with seven floors being underground. The building encompasses two city blocks and can at any time during the day have around ten thousand people inside.

The lights from the prison barely penetrate the film covering my windows as I roll pass it on my left. I've only been in that facility on a few occasions, and I'd prefer those being the only times.

Headquarters is a block later on my right, the CSB initials draping down the sides of the building in a bright hologram. I continue on Lange pass Streman, then turn right into the entrance of the CSB parking garage. The metal arm holds me at bay until the cameras recognize my license plate, then rises, allowing me entry. Even given the late hour I don't find an empty spot until I'm on the fourth level.

After shutting the car off, I make my way down one of the staircases in the corner, then cross the street and enter the building. I have to first pass through the metal detector, which I set off, but the guard on duty knows me and waves me through. The elevators are kept in a core in the center of the structure behind four reception desks, which you must pass to gain access. When they aren't manned, the biometrics for the building are activated, so I place my palm on the reader. The red light on the device turns green, causing the gates to swing open. Before I get onto an elevator I check one of the monitors adhered to the metal plating of the core to see who's keeping me company.

There are only a few detectives for the robbery and SVU divisions, and even though they're on the same floor as I am I rarely ever see them. I check for Frank's name, but I'm not surprised when I don't see it listed. Bastard is probably still at home in his nice, warm bed. I push the button to call the elevator, then select floor six after it arrives. Stepping off, I go to the left and around the core to enter homicide's section. I breeze pass the waiting room since it's empty and head right for my workstation in the far-right corner. The lights automatically come on as they're motion activated. After hanging my wet jacket on the chair for the desk beside mine, I place my gun in a locked drawer, turn on my computer screens, and begin a new file on my victim. There isn't much for me to do until I get her microchip from the coroner, so I take the time searching her name through government databases as well as CSB's private ones.

Lesley Marsh had a hard life, but who of us in Asmor haven't? She dropped out of school at sixteen when her parents died in a murder/suicide. Her first job was at the now defunct club Temptation. They were known for hiring underaged girls to work the poles and booths, which is why they're closed. The ERC, better known as the Entertainment Regulatory Commission, will permit a lot in Nok, except allowing anyone under twenty-one inside as a patron or anyone under eighteen to work a club, bar, or any venue will automatically cause them to lose their license to operate.

After Temptation closed, she worked a couple of part-time jobs as a waitress in several different restaurants until she turned eighteen, then she was back in the night scene and began working at Club Deviant. She's been arrested a few times for possession, which isn't uncommon for strippers and escorts. They'll ingest anything to take the edge off of having to fuck the creeps who pay for their service. There are several women at Verdigris who swallow, snort, or even inject themselves just to get through the night. Some drug use is legal, but only in Nok. Lesley's arrests were in Berrin where she lived. The same can be said for prostitution and gambling: legal in Nok, but nowhere else. Not that it doesn't happen in the other sectors. You'll either get fined or serve time in prison if you're caught.

Looking at the time, I notice it's close to four. Going to visit Lesley's boss, a man named Luke Cobb, will have to wait until later when the club opens. I send him an automated message to his work voicemail with my information and the purpose for my call, giving him my office number in hopes he'll call me back so I don't have to chase him down. My next step is sending a request up to the surveillance group dedicated to the Range sector located on the twenty-fourth floor asking them to pull footage from cameras around the convenience store. I don't know what else I can do at this early hour, so I save my work before going up to the fourteenth floor where the lounges are, and grab a blanket from one of the cabinets before crashing on a couch to get some much-needed sleep.

"Hey, sleeping beauty, get your ass up," Frank's voice pierces through my dreams.

"Fuck off," I grouse, rolling away from him.

"Lloyd's across the street waiting for you."

"What time is it?"

"Eight."

"How'd you know I was up here?" I grumble, tossing off the blanket.

"Because I know you too well. When Lloyd couldn't get ahold of you on your cell phone he called me. It didn't take long to figure out where you disappeared to after seeing your coat hanging on Foster's chair and the late hour I called you."

"I need coffee."

"They have that over there."

Leaving Frank behind, I take the elevator down to the main floor, cross the street, and enter the lobby for the coroner's office. The receptionist isn't in yet, so I go through the waiting room and enter my digital code into a panel by the door that leads toward the exam rooms. Lloyd's assistant, Taylor, is rounding the corner, probably after the sensor in the building indicated someone had entered.

"You look like shit," she says.

"I just woke up," I retort. "Which room is he in?"

"Four. I'll bring you some coffee."

I follow her back around the corner she emerged from. She disappears into the breakroom as we pass it on our right while I continue down the hallway to exam room four at the end on the left. I hate this part of the job, especially the smells that permeate the room and linger in my nostrils and clothes for the rest of the day, though I think I'm the only one who can smell it on me. Lloyd Rhemick is hunched over my victim's body as she lies on the exam table gutted from stem to stern. He's tall, somewhere in his early forties with short, black hair and chiseled features giving him high cheekbones and a slightly pointed nose. He's the night shift coroner, is extremely smart, and arrogant most of the time. He lives in Waterside, so I'm baffled why he chose this profession to go into as there really isn't any money to be made in dead bodies—unless you're a mortician or work for a company that specializes in organ harvesting.

"It's about damn time," he snaps. "I was beginning to think I was going to have to wait for you all day."

11

"Good morning to you, too, Lloyd," I growl. "Where's her chip?"

"Over there," he answers, nodding toward a table by the door. "Her cause of death was exsanguination. The carotid was severed, which isn't a surprise given her wound. What I did find interesting were ligature marks on both her ankles and wrists." He steps to the end of the table, picks up one of her legs, and focuses the light onto the bruises so I can see them better. "From what I can tell the possible material used is some type of rope given the abrasions it left behind. Her skin is raw around the edging of the bruises, so she may have tried to free herself from her constraints," he explains. "She also had lividity in her chest and stomach, so she was facing down when she died and was left in that position for a while."

"The officers found her lying on her back, so she was more than likely dumped at the convenience store. Do you have time of death?"

"Her life ended somewhere between Saturday night and Sunday morning," he answers just as Taylor joins us, carrying a mug of coffee for me.

"Did you get the number off her breast implants?"

"How'd you know she had those?" Lloyd asks, surprised.

"It's not hard to notice fake breasts. They're not supposed to point up when you're lying down," I reply, which causes Taylor to snicker.

"I sent that information to the evidence technicians already. Taylor, pull up the photos from the scene."

She steps over to the smart screen, tapping its surface, and scrolling through the files until she finds the one labeled with my victim's name. Lloyd stays at the table while I go and stand beside Taylor, reviewing the images as I haven't looked at them yet. The first few photos show Lesley spread eagle on the pavement like she was when I arrived, only the ground is dry; the rain hadn't started yet. I tap on one of the pictures, expanding it to get a better view of her face and torso. A knot forms in my stomach when I realize there's an inconsistency between what I'm seeing and how Lloyd described her possible manner of death.

"Did you look at these?" I ask, turning toward him as he continues to work.

"Of course I did," he grouses.

"There isn't a spot of blood on her other than what's around her wound. If she was lying face down as she bled to death most of her should've been covered in blood."

"Not unless the killer cleaned her before placing her for you to find."

"Did you run a chemical panel on her skin to see if a specific cleanser was used?"

"I'm not stupid, Olivia. Of course I did and it came back negative, along with the rape kit. She did have sex just before she died, but it was more than likely consensual given where she worked. I didn't find any semen, so they used protection. I'm still waiting for toxicology though."

"Then where's the blood?" Taylor asks.

"Could it be at the place where she was killed?" Lloyd counters, being a smartass. He chuckles when she scrunches up her face in annoyance.

"Hopefully I'll have that location when I get her tracking records from the Hub," I say.

My comment causes Taylor to shiver. "I hate that CSB can trace everyone's movements."

"How else do you maintain safety?" Lloyd asks. "And keep those who shouldn't be roaming freely behind bars or in their shithole apartments? It's not like those of us in Waterside are treated any differently than those on the mainland. Our movements are recorded as well, as they should be."

"That's your opinion," she says.

"I'll just take my CSB ass back to the office." I hand Taylor the mug to avoid being pulled into an argument these two have a little too often. "Let me know when the toxicology results come in."

I grab the small baggy with the microchip secured inside and return to the office, but I don't go to my workstation. Instead, I head up to the evidence labs located on the nineteenth floor to borrow one of their microscopes so I can read the serial number on the chip as they all have one. The smell of harsh chemicals hits me before I've even stepped off the elevator and it causes my throat to burn and my eyes to water. I should've made Hayden come down to my desk instead of me searching for him in the labyrinth of machines, workstations, computers, and chemical baths. I spot his mange of wild brown hair bobbing through the aisles, heading toward his office in the back, so I practically sprint in his direction to get away from the obnoxious fumes.

"You don't have to come up here, you know," he says, laughing as he closes the door behind me.

"How can you stand it?" I ask, taking a seat in front of his desk as he moves around to the other side.

"I lost my sense of smell years ago," he replies. "What can I help you with?"

I hand him the evidence bag. "Can you get the serial number off this for me?"

"Sure, just give me a minute."

He breaks the seal with a small knife, then removes the chip with a pair of tweezers before turning around and placing it on the stage of the microscope he keeps on top of a filing cabinet behind his desk. I grab a small pad of paper and a pen since I left my tablet down in my desk.

"Ready?" he asks.

"Go ahead."

"LM-0714-1127."

"Thanks."

He places the chip back into its bag, adding a new seal, which he initials before returning it to me. "Is this for the body that was found early this morning?"

"Yes. The case got thrown my way. Were your technicians able to find anything at the scene?"

"No. It had all been washed away by the rain. Any evidence you're going to get will have to come from the body itself, or whatever you might find in her apartment or work."

"Great," I grumble, sighing. "Send me the tox report when it's available as well as the information on her implants."

"Sure."

I go back to the sixth floor, which is swarming with detectives, officers, and supervisors like any typical Monday morning. Foster scowls at me as I'd left my jacket on his chair, but it's now hanging on the coat rack in the corner where I should've put it in the first place. I sit down, add notes to the file, and send off the serial number to the CSB contact at the Hub. Before placing the microchip into my locked drawer, I study the tiny cylinder very carefully. Entire lives are recorded, tracked, and monitored on this small device. It's implanted under our skin on our right wrist at the age of thirteen when we can legally start working. Each chip is unique to its owner, including the serial number, which is derived from our initials, birth day and month, then ending with the time we were born. Only those who work in the CSB know how the numbers are created, but I'm sure some people have figured it out—if they even realize there's a number to begin with.

The CSB and the central government for our country known as Leyon decided to add the number after counterfeit chips were discovered being sold and used for those willing to pay the high price of anonymity. Altering the chip, removing it, or manipulating its programming is punishable with several years in prison, though hardly anyone ever gets caught or serves time. The main culprits now are minors trying to gain access to the clubs. They'll pay some flunky a few hundred dollars to change their birth information, but it's never very good and highly noticeable—at least to me.

My stomach begins to growl, so I head up to the ninth floor where the breakroom is with its various food stations. I get in line with everyone else and proceed to order an omelet, fresh fruit, and orange juice. After paying for my food and grabbing utensils from a cart along the corner, I take a seat at an empty table by one of the many televisions dangling down from the ceiling or adhered to the walls. I ignore what's being broadcasted as it's mainly morning talk shows everyone likes to watch, but I hate. The phone in my back pocket begins to chime, so I remove it, selecting the audio only option when I notice the name on the screen.

"I need you to work tonight," Joe says, his voice perky as always.

"Why? I had a homicide fall in my lap earlier this morning, so I'm not going to be available for at least the next few days."

"Liv, I have a client who wants to hire you." I can sense the smile on his face. "He's only available to meet tonight before heading out of town on business. I promise once the meeting is over you can go home."

"Did your client mention what he or she is hiring me for?"

"It's a missing persons case, but that's all I know."

"And I have to come in dressed for work?"

"Yes, because I'm not sure what time he'll be showing and I could use you on the floor."

"Am I waitressing or bartending?"

"Bartending, so be at the club by eight."

"I'll see you then."

Ending the call, I slip the phone into my pocket as I finish my meal. When I'm back at my workstation, I remove my gun, securing the holster to my waist, grab my jacket, and reach Hayden on the phone, telling him to have a team meet me at Lesley's apartment in an hour. I remember to grab my tablet, which I put in a leather satchel, cinching it around my shoulders before making my way to the elevator. After retrieving my car, I turn left onto Lange out of the parking garage, then make an immediate right onto Streman. Roscow Apartments sit off the intersection of Streman and Twenty-Second Street in Berrin right on the edge with Nok sector. Normally I would call the manager of the complex to advise him or her I'm coming, but I know the man who runs these particular apartments because it's the same ones my father lives in.

There are four buildings in the complex, each standing eight-stories and containing ten apartments per floor. The buildings surround a dilapidated courtyard with two playgrounds filled with rusted swings and slides, plots of dead gardens, and a grill pit. I pull into the parking lot for building A since that's where the manager lives and make sure to lock my car as the neighborhood is known for its thieves. The lock on the entrance is broken, so the door pulls open without an issue. In the entryway are countless mailboxes housed in the wall with scratch marks, dents, or simply open spilling their contents. I reach the end, turn right, and stop at the first door on my left. I lean my ear against the warped wood before knocking, noticing the high volume of the television as a game show plays. It takes a few minutes for the raps on the door to register with the occupant on the other side.

"Olivia, what are you doing here?" Randy Lok, the complex's manager, asks after he opens the door.

"Can I come in? I need to talk to you."

He steps aside, then closes the door after I've entered before returning to his recliner by the television and turning down the volume while I sit on the couch. Randy is somewhere in his sixties with almond-shaped features, olive-toned skin, and balding gray hair. He keeps an eye on my father when I'm not able to, which is often as I still have a difficult time understanding the person he's turned into over the last several decades.

"What's up?" Randy asks in his usual cheerful manner.

"You have a tenant named Lesley Marsh, correct?"

"She's over in building C. Why?"

"She was killed over the weekend."

"I'm not surprised," he says. "I knew she was going to get into trouble one day with the type of people she hung out with. Which includes your dad."

"What?" I ask, dismayed.

"He and Lesley were an on and off item for a few months. I think he was the one providing her with the drugs she got caught with a while back. If anyone is going to be upset she's gone it'll be him."

I shiver at the thought of him sleeping with someone nearly nine years younger than me, forty years his junior. This is one of the reasons I don't talk to him. I should let Frank know of my father's possible involvement since he'll probably want to pull me off the case given my closeness to it, but I have no intention of telling him. I've never been removed from an investigation and I'm not about to make this my first one.

"Do you have a key? I need to go through her things and let the evidence technicians into her apartment," I say, getting to my feet.

"Sure." Reaching into a drawer in the end table next to his recliner, he removes several key rings, each one labeled with the building and tenant information. He hands me the ring for building C. "Just bring it back when you're done."

I thank him, then return to my car to drive around the complex. I shouldn't have to worry about running into my father at the moment as he lives in building D and sleeps mainly during the day because he works nights in one of the industrial parks in Crer sector. Lesley's apartment is 8B, and since the building doesn't have a working elevator I have to use the stairs to climb all eight stories. Thankfully her door is right across from the staircase, so after rifling through the keys I unlock the door and let myself in.

The apartment isn't very big. The living room and kitchen are crammed together while there's a tiny bathroom and bedroom off to the left. Trash, clothing, dirty dishes, and discarded towels cover the floor and furnishings. Mold is growing on food remnants left in the sink and the trashcan is overflowing. I step carefully over everything, working my way to the bedroom, making sure not to touch anything until forensics gets here with gloves. The sheets on the bed are rumpled and there's at least one used condom discarded on the floor with a few more in the trash in the bathroom.

"Olivia," my name reverberates in the small space.

"I'm back here, Hayden," I reply.

He joins me carrying a pair of gloves, handing them to me. "Where do you want my guys to start?"

"Have them tackle the living room and kitchen while you and I work in here."

He steps out of the room briefly as I put on the gloves and begin going through her dresser drawers. Hayden returns with evidence bags, labels, and more gloves. I let him collect the condoms and any other biological fluid we come across, which the bed is loaded with, making me wonder if she's ever changed the sheets. I place them into an evidence bag, seal it, and write my initials and the case number on the label. I then move into the bathroom where I find a couple of toothbrushes in the holder on the sink, adding those to our growing pile. The two of us finish up around three, so I tell Hayden to return the keys to the manager, take everything back to the lab for his team to process, and to seal off the apartment as I'm heading home for the day.

I'm exhausted, in desperate need of a shower, and I still have to work tonight. When I turn the corner for my street I become instantly aggravated by the car I notice parked out front. I grumble under my breath as the garage door rises and I back the Nimbus inside, angry that my peaceful few hours at home are no longer going to happen. The moment I enter my house, the sounds of a woman begging to be fucked fills the air. From the door into the garage I see a porno playing larger than life on my television as a beefy arm is draped over the couch.

"You do have your own place," I begin, heading toward Dean. "Why are you here?"

"Because your screen is better than mine," he replies, gesturing at the television.

"Why aren't you at work?"

"I'm off today. Where have you been?"

"At work," I say. "And I'm due at the club later. Leave so I can sleep."

"What part are you playing?" he asks, salivating.

"Not the one you want me to. I'm bartending. Besides, I fuck you for free. Why would you want to go to the club and pay for it?"

19

"I'd pay anything to see you in one of those outfits," he says, grabbing me around the waist. "I know you have two of them somewhere in your closet. Maybe you'll wear them for me one day."

"Only in my nightmares," I retort, pulling away from him.

I despise the clothes Joe makes all the women wear, but his club isn't the only one that forces its workers to be barely covered as drunk men drool over them. The only people who get to dress decently are the bouncers. There are two different styles of dress at Verdigris: a mini dress made of fishnet with the sides cutout from just under the armpit to the tops of the thighs, thin leather bands crisscrossing over the exposed skin. A thong is the only under garment as nothing else is to adorn the outfit, so your tits are in full view of the world. I, on the other hand, use pasties since I'm not in to showing off everything I have to the general public.

The other garment is a leather bikini with mesh cups for the bra, thin leather straps holding the top around the neck and connecting it to the bottom, which is simply a thong with snaps for easy access to the goods. Each outfit is color-coded for the type of job you're handling. For the mini dress: black is for the bartenders, blue are for the waitresses, and white means you're working the service counter at the door. For the bikini: green stands for lap dancers and red is for the escorts. The strippers choose their own clothes since they aren't in them for very long. Every woman at the club is issued one uniform of each color and design as we're meant to be universal during our employment. I flat out refuse to wear the bikini and the only reason Joe lets me get away with that is because of the extra work I do for his friends and clients.

"I'm going to bed," I say. "Just clean up whatever mess you leave behind when you're done."

After closing my bedroom door, I take off everything except my bra and panty, then get under the covers. I begin to doze off when I hear the door open followed by the bed shaking. Dean rolls me onto my back, his naked body pressed against me. His fingers glide their way under my panty, fondling me as his mouth covers mine while his other hand works on removing my bra. His mouth moves to my breast as his fingers penetrate me, causing me to moan. He suckles as his thumb brushes gently against my clitoris, his fingers sliding in and out. I reach a point where I orgasm, my eyes rolling into the back of my head. Dean almost rips off my panties so he can fuck me as I hear the woman from the television cry out in pleasure.

Two

As Dean lies passed out in bed I make myself a quick dinner before getting into the shower. I toss the black mini dress in my travel bag along with a makeup kit, high-heeled shoes, cell phone, my CSB credentials, wallet, and gun. There's no way in hell I wear that outfit in public other than inside of the club. I can't ride my motorcycle while in it either. When I step into the garage, I open the door at the end on the right, my Rune sitting there waiting for me. It's the latest in speed cycles. The handles are close to the front wheel, so I practically lie across the machine to ride it. The tires are wide for better grip, the seat a nice soft leather, and the foot rests are by the back wheel. I grab my helmet from its hook on the wall, secure my bag across my back before donning the helmet, and turn the motorcycle on with a simple push of a button. It's easy to start because of the technology in the helmet, which houses all the motorcycle's information, my speedometer, and the access code to turn on the bike. You can't start a Rune without its appropriate helmet, making them nearly impossible to steal.

I slowly move out of the garage, then close the door, but I don't activate the alarm for the house because Dean is still inside and I don't need him setting it off when he leaves… if he does leave. I have to travel through Hunnat sector to reach Nok and traffic is heavy at this time of night since everyone is returning home from work. I take Lange over the river that encircles the entertainment sector from the rest and am immediately greeted with eye-piercing neon signs, scantily-clad dressed women, and roads so narrow that only one vehicle at a time can fit down them. The buildings along the sectors outer edge are close together, some almost sitting atop their neighbor. These are where the smaller clubs, porn shops, tattoo parlors, smoke dens, gambling rooms, and food dives live. The rest of the area opens up a little more the deeper you go.

Due to how densely compacted everything in Nok is, CSB uses round, bulbous drones to patrol the streets. Each drone has roughly twenty cameras and zip up and down the alleys and streets documenting everything it sees, sending the feeds back to not only

CSB Station 5, but also to the sector's surveillance floor at headquarters. The officers don't want to leave their comfortable nest until they're forced to, especially when many of the patrons of this sector view the officers as an interference, not a safety measure. A drone darts over my head, happily making its way around as if it was a living object. The streets begin to gradually widen as the establishments become larger. I turn right onto Chestnut, then head down the alley behind the club a few blocks later. After parking my bike with a handful of other vehicles, I turn off the engine, and make my way inside by way of the back door.

I go down the hallway until the end, then turn right and head toward Joe's office, but he's not there when I crack open the door. I proceed to the opposite end where the dressing room is along with several girls getting ready.

"Liv, I wasn't expecting to see you tonight," one says, sitting at the makeup counter while I go toward the lockers.

"Joe asked me to come in," I reply.

"You look exhausted," another comments. "Rough day at the office or at home?"

"Both," I answer, opening the locker with my name stenciled on it.

"New case?"

"Yeah," I mumble. "A girl who works at Club Deviant was murdered over the weekend."

"Which is one of the reasons I love working here," the young woman at the makeup counter says. "Everyone knows not to fuck with Joe's girls when a homicide detective works here and will fuck them up if they even try to cause the littlest bit of trouble."

The few who are in the room chuckle at the comment.

"What was her name?"

"Lesley Marsh," I answer as I begin to disrobe, shoving my clothes into the locker.

"She doesn't sound familiar," another one chimes in.

The conversation ends, allowing me to slip on the thong and place my sparkling silver pasties over my tits before donning the mini dress. I strap the high heels around my calves, brush my hair, put on makeup, and lock my locker before heading back into the hallway and through a set of double doors that'll take me to the club floor.

Bright lights fill the space as everyone is busy preparing for our patrons. Once they arrive, the white lights will be replaced by colorful neon, darkening the club to give it a perverted feel. I flip the partition on the countertop over to enter the bar so I can take stock in what we have and what I'll need to grab from storage by Joe's office. The mat that covers the floor is sticky like always and many of the glasses weren't cleaned from the night before. I'll have to take care of those since it's obvious no one else will, including the cleaning crew that's supposed to come through here every morning. I take my list and head into the back, grabbing one of the bouncers to help carry the crates of booze while I handle the bags of pretzels and peanuts, which is the only food we serve. I'm busy stocking the shelves under the countertop when I spot Joe lingering on the other side.

"Good, you're here," he says, smiling while some of his graying, sandy hair falls over his face. "My client should be here around midnight. I'll have the two of you discuss business in my office and away from prying eyes."

"He can't get here any sooner?" I ask, grumbling at the late hour.

"There's some things he needs to wrap up before he leaves Asmor. I'll be back in a little while as I have to pick up Henry from the rail station down the street."

Joe disappears from view while I continue to crouch on the floor, my knees hurting from being in this position. Of all the club owners Joe Ambrose is by far the oldest—and the wealthiest. He stands six-foot-two and has an amazingly firm body for someone in his early sixties. He treats all his employees fairly, for the most part, and is almost like a grandfather to the younger ones. He's never violated a law, and I make sure his business stays in compliance by keeping an eye out for anyone who looks too young to be in here and has somehow made it past the initial scan to verify their identification. One of the young women from earlier named Alice, who's a skinny

24

girl with bright red hair, joins me behind the bar and the two of us work on cleaning up the station. We bitch and complain about the crew from the night before as the DJ starts his speakers, lights, and volume checks from his booth between us and the stage where the strippers perform.

Alice and I are premixing some of the drinks when Joe returns with his best friend, Henry, an elderly man in his mid-seventies. He's a regular and never has to pay for a drink, though he only consumes club soda. Joe brings him in as often as possible to get the elderly man out of the small, ratty apartment he once shared with his wife of fifty years before she passed away last year. He's a big flirt with all the young women, but he's completely harmless and we all love seeing his soft, gentle face. Joe places him on his normal stool by the partition for the countertop before heading to the main entrance.

"My love is here," Henry says, reaching toward me.

I lean over the bar to give him a kiss. "Hi, Henry. Do you want your usual?"

"Yes, please."

I pour him a club soda, adding a slice of lime before placing it on the counter in front of him.

"Joe tells me you've got a new case," he says after swallowing a small sip. "Is it intriguing? Do you know who did it?"

"Not yet, Henry, but I'll let you know when I capture the culprit."

He smiles and winks at Alice, striking up a conversation with her as the lights change, the music begins to blare, the escorts go stand before their assigned rooms, the waitresses take to the floor with their trays, the strippers to the stage in their lingerie, and the bouncers to their positions around the floor and over by the entrances as the club opens. It's not long before the tables and booths to fill up, the drink orders coming in faster than Alice and I can make them. Henry chats up a couple of the waitresses when they come by along with a few of the strippers after they're done performing. I glance around the room during a brief lull, noticing almost all of the private pods where the escorts perform their tricks have been turned so the back wall of the booth is facing out, hindering the rest of the club from seeing what's going on behind the red drapes that cover the now-obstructed doorways.

"How much do I need to pay Joe to get you in one of those?" Dean asks, pointing to the pods while taking a seat at the bar.

"What the hell are you doing here?"

"I was lonely at your place."

"Then go back to your apartment, or bother one of your other female friends so they'll take pity on you. I'm busy."

"You need to wear that outfit for me someday," he says, licking his lips.

"You've already seen me naked."

"Yeah, but guys love a woman in uniform."

"What do you want to drink?" I ask, rolling my eyes.

"A beer."

I pour him one from the tap, then scroll through the sales screen under the countertop for his seat to create his account. Each stool, table, and booth has one, and only the employees have access to them. As I wipe down the counter I notice a green 'X' stamped on the back of his hand, which indicates he's here for a lap dance and to see the strippers. Each guest has to pay for the type of entertainment they're seeking before they can get past the main entrance into the club. The stamps are color-coded just like the outfits, but with only black, green, and red as available options.

"Why are you sitting here if you paid to watch the strippers and get a lap dance?" I ask, pouring beer into several glasses for a waitress, who eyes Dean nervously.

"I'm checking out my options before selecting a spot to sit and a woman to pleasure me," he replies, smiling. "Besides, all the tables and booths are taken."

"Olivia," Joe's voice cuts through the noise like a knife. He glares at Dean while he stands beside Henry. "I need you in the office."

"Sure." I dry my hands on a towel as a new girl comes to take my place.

"Bye, doll." Henry kisses my cheek.

"I'll be seeing you, Henry."

Joe wraps my arm around his as he escorts me off the floor and to his office, but he doesn't open the door right away.

"What's Dean doing here?" he asks, scowling.

"Drinking," I reply, being a smartass.

"I want you to take him with you when you leave. He's bad for business."

"Fine," I reply, rolling my eyes.

Joe's never liked Dean, especially when he's had to have him thrown out of the club a couple of times. It's not because he's a CSB officer, but because he can become violent if he's been drinking too much. That's another reason why I'm infuriated he's here. I hate babysitting the fucker when he's intoxicated and that's exactly what will happen if he's not gone by the time I'm done. My night just got even longer.

I follow Joe into his office, which is dimly lit because of the thirty monitors he has adhered to the wall showing every inch of the club, including the private pods that are in use. These same security feeds are being viewed in the office by the vestibule between the main and street entrances. There's also a containment cell there for those who can't hold their liquor or their women. Joe's desk is positioned diagonally from the back corner, affording him a full view the monitors. A tall, older man possibly in his late-fifties with graying blond hair stands at my approach, having been seated in front of the desk.

"Olivia, this is Richard Cassidy," Joe says, introducing us. "Why don't you two talk while I go keep an eye on the floor."

Before I can protest, Joe closes the door. I become very self-conscious by how Richard is leering at me in my very revealing getup, so I go and sit in Joe's seat behind the desk, folding my arms to cover my chest and crossing my legs at the knee.

"What can I do for you, Mr. Cassidy?" I ask after a few moments of awkward silence.

"Please call me Richard," he says, flashing a smile that makes my skin crawl. "I'm hoping you can assist me in finding my daughter."

"How long has she been missing?"

"A little over two weeks."

"Why not go to CSB if she's been gone that long?"

"Because I've been told you'd handle it discreetly where CSB is known for their less than candid attitude when it comes to delving into people's private lives. Especially those from my circle of society."

"I'm sure Joe told you I'm a homicide detective with CSB."

"Yes, and you come highly recommended by others of my caliber. Your boss being one of them."

"Do you have any insight as to where your daughter might have gone? Does she run with a tough crowd? Is she a partier? Into the drug scene?"

"Brooke is definitely a partier. I wouldn't be surprised if she's hiding in one of the clubs, bars, or smoke dens in this sector."

"You probably have the type of money that can easily afford you a private investigator. What made you select me?"

"As I said before, Ms. Darrow, you come highly recommended by everyone you've worked for," Richard replies, his tone sending shivers down my spine as I can only imagine what he's heard about me. "Also, the investigators I know are greedy bastards who spend their allowances on drinking and women instead of what they were paid to do."

I think about my homicide victim. "Do you have a picture of your daughter?"

He reaches into his coat pocket, extracting his cell phone. After scrolling through several images he finally hands the device to me. The young woman on the screen looks nothing like the girl from this morning, which brings me relief. The daughter has blond hair like her father and is posed in a string bikini to show off her thin body as she lounges beside a pool, grinning wide for the camera. It's an odd photo for a father to be carrying, which makes me wonder what kind of relationship they have.

"How old is she?" I ask, returning the phone.

"She's twenty-two."

"Is she your only child?"

"No. I have a son, Kane, who's thirty-four. My children share different mothers. I married Brooke's after my first wife died."

"Where's Brooke's mother now?"

"Buried far up north with her wretched family," he replies, sounding smug. "The bitch overdosed a year after Brooke was born. That's what I get for knocking up a worthless piece of trash. My housekeeper raised the girl for me as I was busy building my company."

"Is Brooke known for running away? Do you think someone may have taken her?"

"She's always throwing tantrums. Particularly when she doesn't get her way. This isn't the first time she's disappeared, but it has been the longest, which is what concerns me."

"Do you have a list of her friends and the clubs she's known to frequent?"

"I'll have my secretary send all that over to you tomorrow as I leave on business in a few hours."

"Where are you traveling to?"

"Hillcrest."

"That's in Whitmond, isn't it?"

"Yes. I have a convention to attend and will be away for the rest of the week."

"What do you do for a living?"

"I own BluTrend Technologies. We create state of the art microtechnology like the chip in your wrist," he says, pointing to my arm. "My son is the CFO, so I'll give you his number to contact in my absence."

29

"Did Joe give you my information?"

"No, he hasn't," Richard replies, grinning.

I reach into the top drawer where Joe keeps business cards he made up for me that don't contain my CSB credentials, listing just my cell phone number and personal email address. I hand the card over to Richard, who passes his along to me after writing his son's number on the back, but I have no place to currently put it.

"I'll make sure you receive what you need by morning," he says, rising from his seat.

"I can't guarantee how much time I'll be able to put into this because of my primary job."

"I know, but I have every confidence in you, Olivia."

He smiles, which causes the corners of his eyes to crease, then leaves by way of Joe's private entrance off the alley after shaking my hand. I go to the dressing room to put away the card and change, but before I can loosen my heels Alice comes in stating Joe needs me to finish out the night since Dean has made himself at home in one of the booths. I shake my head, roll my eyes, and follow Alice back to the bar where Joe is sitting beside Henry.

"He's asking for you," Joe says, narrowing his eyes at Dean, who's leaning over his table ogling the women on stage and those parading around the floor.

"How much has he had to drink?"

"Alice?" Joe asks.

"Ten beers in under a half hour," she replies.

"God damn it," I utter. "Call him a cab. I'll work on getting him out the back door."

Joe pats me on the shoulder, then heads to his office while I make my way over to the last booth far against the wall. Dean smiles as I sit across from him, an empty stein in his hand.

"Where have you been?" he asks, his demeanor turning nasty.

"Why the fuck does it matter? I was on break."

"Is that why Joe has been out here watching me like a hawk? I know he can do it from the comfort of his office, which makes me wonder where you really were and what you've been doing."

"What the fuck is wrong with you? I was in back on break. I can't help it if Joe was out here instead of his office."

"Then why did he need to see you if he was only going to be gone for a few minutes while you've been absent for almost a half hour? I want to know what you were doing, Liv," Dean demands, his voice and temper rising.

"Knock this shit off," I snap, slapping him on the arm. "You're drunk. Let's leave before you get into trouble."

"I'm already in trouble," he retorts.

"What do you mean?"

"I've been suspended," he gripes, slamming the stein down onto the table, drawing a few people's attention.

"Why?" I ask, trying to sound shocked when in reality I'm not. Dean has always walked a thin line with being an officer. It was only a matter of time before it caught up to him.

"My supervisor didn't like it when I told him to shove his opinion up his ass, then I punched him."

"Why the hell did you do that?"

"He was going to assign me to desk duty because I got too forceful with a drug dealer I arrested last week in Vale. I kept telling him the guy rammed his own head into my car door. I can't help it his neck broke."

"You killed him?" I ask, this time genuinely stunned.

"No. He's just paralyzed."

"Fuck, Dean. Why would you do something so stupid?"

"It wasn't stupid!" he hollers, which draws every bouncer on the floor our way. "What the hell do you want?" Dean hisses as they stand in front of us.

"It's time for you to leave, Mr. Morgan," one of the bouncers replies, his muscles stretching his thin shirt beyond comfort.

31

"I'm not going anywhere," he says, seething.

"Dean, let me take you home." I remove the stein from his grasp, so he can't use it as a weapon.

"Only if you go with me."

"Sure, I'll go with you," I say, trying to placate him. "Where did you park your car?"

"Down the street," he replies, reaching into his pocket to hand me the keys.

"Let's go."

I work on pulling him from the booth as the bouncers give us room. Wrapping my arm around his waist, I guide him toward the door that'll take us to the back hallway. I have him halfway across the floor when I hear someone catcall behind me and I instantly know the owner of the voice.

"Fuck, Darrow. I've never seen you look better," Glen Growsky says, smacking my ass as I pass his table. I hadn't noticed he was there. "Looks good on you. I wouldn't mind seeing it on the floor of my bedroom either. Maybe when you're done with Dean it'll be my turn."

Dean shoves me to the floor as he swings at Glen, his fist making contact with Glen's face, knocking the man out of his chair. The bouncers work on controlling the situation while I try to get between the two, which is a mistake. Glen places his arms on my hips and works on lifting off my dress. Dean grabs my arm, throwing me aside before seizing Glen by the throat and hurtling him across the room, knocking over several tables and patrons. One of the bouncers takes a syringe from his belt, plunging the needle into Dean's neck. It takes a few seconds for the sedative to kick in, and Dean collapses to the floor. Joe put this measure in place after another incident we had with a patron. They're much easier to handle when they're unconscious. The bouncers drag Dean out the back door to the waiting cab as I follow behind them, nursing a sore elbow and shoulder.

"Take him to Trinity Heights in Berrin. Bungalow number 27," I tell the cab driver.

I shove Dean's keys into his pocket, remove his wallet, and hand over every dollar inside to the driver before heading back into the club, but I don't go to the floor. Instead, I make my way the bathroom to have a look at myself. My hair is a mess, my makeup smudged, and a bruise is beginning to form on my arm where I landed on the floor. Joe's waiting for me in the hallway when I exit.

"He's banned for life!" Joe raves. "This was the last straw, Olivia. I don't want that asshole in this establishment ever again."

"Don't worry, he won't be," I snap, then turn to head for the dressing room when Joe stops me.

"Where the hell do you think you're going? You need to clean up the mess he made out there and finish working your shift."

"You said I could leave when he did?" I utter, stunned, gesturing toward the door.

"That was before he turned my club into a fighting arena." Joe takes several deep breaths to calm himself down. "I know you didn't want him here anymore than I did, but his actions just lost me customers for the night, thereby costing me money."

"I'll have him pay you for the loss."

"That's not what I want and he can't afford it. Friday night you're working the pods."

"No fucking way! I quit."

"And how will you pay for the luxuries you've become fond of owning? You'd make a hell of lot more money in the pods or on the floor as a lap dancer than you'll ever see being a bartender or a waitress."

"No, Joe. That isn't going to happen. You can find yourself another detective to help your friends when they're too stubborn and arrogant to go to CSB directly."

"How about we make a deal?" he says, realizing I'm not going to back down and he can't afford to lose me, especially when his clients are involved. "Finish out tonight, and Friday I'll have you waitress, but you'll need to wear the escort outfit. I have several of them in blue so no one will confuse you with the women working the pods or as a lap dancer. Your tips will more than double, especially if you let the customers fondle you a little like the others do."

"You can't be serious?"

"It's either that or I tell Frank Corro you're fucking Dean, which is a violation of your job."

"I'm going to kill him," I growl.

"Well if you do I'll help you hide the body," Joe says, trying to get me to laugh at the uncomfortable predicament I'm now facing.

"Fine, whatever. Just let me fix my hair and face, then I'll return to the floor."

He pats me on the check before heading into his office. I make my way to the dressing room where I run a comb through my mane and touch up the spots that were smudged. When I step back into the club most of the tables have been righted and are now filled with new patrons. I carefully look around for Glen, spotting him in a booth, his eye beginning to swell. I step over to the bar, pour him a beer, then take it over as a peace offering.

"Where's Dean?" he asks, accepting the drink.

"He's gone home," I reply, then turn to leave.

Glen grabs my arm, stopping me. "What's your rush, Darrow? According to your boss you're mine for the evening."

"Like hell I am." I yank out of his grip. As I turn to walk away, I notice Joe has emerged from the back and is glaring at me from across the room, nodding his head for me to stay where I am.

My blood boils as I feel my face reddening. Glen wraps an arm around my waist, pulling me into the booth beside him. He adjusts our positions, so we're only noticeable to the women on stage, their dead eyes staring into a void I wish I could see. His hands wander my body, tugging at the mini dress while his mouth tastes my neck. He notices the exploding star I have tattooed on my right hip, which is visible through the leather straps and fishnet.

"I wonder how many other tattoos you have and if I'll get to see them," he whispers.

34

My skin crawls from his touch, but as I try to wriggle my way free several of the bouncers approach our booth, then stand with their backs to us, blocking our view of everyone, plunging us into near darkness.

"I don't believe this shit," I complain, elbowing Glen in the abdomen.

He hits me across the face. "It's my turn to give the orders, Olivia," he says, his hand seizing the back of my neck.

"You're just loving this, aren't you? I'm sure you can't wait to tell everyone at your station how you had to force a homicide detective to fuck you because no woman in their right mind would ever touch you. Not even your wife."

"When I tell it you'll be a simple whore. No one will know it's you except me. That way I can relive it every chance I get and no one can spoil it."

Unzipping his pants, he exposes is erect cock, then pulls me onto his lap. He pushes my thong aside before penetrating me. His moans fill the air as I grimace. After removing my dress, he takes off the pasties, and suckles my breasts like he's looking for milk to come from them. My nipples become sore and my hips hurt from the way I'm straddling his legs. Glen uses one of his fingers to tease my clitoris while he forces me to ride him. I bite my lip as I begin to climax, my orgasm seizing him in a chokehold.

"I knew you were a good fuck," he says, letting out a loud grunt.

He comes and it drips down my legs. I go to stand, but he holds me in place, his cock still vibrating. He rests his head on my chest as the table I'm leaning against digs into my back. His fingers begin to play with me again and the orgasm is instant as well as long lasting. Glen moans in my ear as he comes again, a sigh of pleasure escaping my lips, though internally I feel only disgust.

"That should make up for tonight." Glen brushes his lips over my stiffened nipples.

He pushes me off and I scramble to put my dress on, though it really doesn't matter now. The bouncers part as he leaves and I stay

35

sitting in the booth, disgusted with myself and everything around me. Alice makes her way over to the booth with a towel in hand.

"Here," she says, sounding downtrodden as she hands it to me. "Joe said you can leave now."

"Thanks," I mumble, embarrassed.

She returns to the bar as I wipe my legs, the floor, and the leather upholstery of the booth. When I'm in the dressing room I toss the towel into a bin by the showers. Dangling in front of my locker is a blue bikini in my size. I tear it off the hanger, shove it in my bag, and quickly change so I can head home. Once there, I drop the bag on the floor of the bedroom, strip out of my clothes, and crawl into the shower stall where I turn on the water to scrub my skin raw and bawl.

Three

An annoying vibrating noise disturbs my sleep. Rolling over to look at the clock, I notice it's just after ten in the morning. The noise stops, but only briefly. I slide out of bed and dig through my bag until I locate my cell phone, which stops ringing. There are over twenty missed calls and dozens of text messages from Dean with the latest being only moments ago. I shut off the device, then head into my living room where I set it in its holder to charge. After making myself a cup of coffee, I snatch my laptop from my desk and sit down on the couch as I have no intention of going into the office today. I turn on the television for background noise while I log into the CSB mainframe to access my files, emails, and databases.

The toxicology report has been updated with no findings, meaning nothing unusual was found in her system. Her implants were part of a batch that were sent to the Boumont Center, which handles plastic surgeries. I'll need to get a subpoena to access their records to find out who paid for them. Checking my email, there's a data recording of Lesley's microchip, and as I launch the program needed to track her precise whereabouts an alert flashes across the television advising me someone is trying to gain access to my home using an outdated code. I know immediately who it is since I changed it before going to bed last night.

"Liv, open the door!" Dean shouts, pounding on the wood frame. "Why isn't the code working?"

I pick up the remote for the cameras that circle my property and call up the one for the front door onto the television.

"Go away, Dean," I utter after activating the voice feature.

"Are you all right? What happened to you last night?" he asks, sounding desperate and scared. "You didn't come home with me like you said you would."

"Leave, Dean," I demand, my voice trembling.

"Not until you talk to me."

I set the laptop on the coffee table, go into my bedroom, and retrieve my gun from the bag I carried last night. After disarming the alarm, I open the door and point the weapon at Dean's startled face.

"Go the fuck away," I say through clenched teeth.

"What happened?" he asks, trying to reach out and touch the welt that developed just under my eye overnight from Glen hitting me.

"You, that's what happened," I reply, my hand shaking as adrenaline pumps heavily through my veins.

"I did that?" he asks, startled by the idea.

"You might as well have."

"Liv, put the gun down and let me come inside so we can talk."

"No, Dean. Go home and leave me the hell alone."

I slam the door in his face, setting the lock in place before he can turn the knob. Going back to the living room, I place the gun on my desk and resume sitting on the couch, but I don't pick up my laptop as I'm trembling horribly. Dean stands confused on my doorstep for a few more minutes before disappearing from view. I turn off the television and head into my bedroom where I change into a swimsuit and put my hair in a ponytail, then step out the back door by the small dining room and onto the patio that surrounds my inground pool.

I swim for what seems like hours, doing laps until every muscle aches and my mind becomes numb. This has always been a respite for me, one I began to use after my mother died. It was the one thing my father permitted me to do outside of going to school as he was terrified to let me out of his sight for too long. That eventually changed when he began drinking and I was left to my own devices. I head back inside, shower, dress, and make myself something to eat before sitting on the couch and turning on the television to watch a movie. It's not long until my peace is disturbed by the ringing of my doorbell. The camera above the threshold automatically goes on, displaying my visitor in the upper corner of the television.

"What now?" I growl as I stand, setting my plate down by my darkened laptop.

Frank looks worried when I open the door, blocking him from entering.

"I'm working from home today," I say before he can utter a word.

"I guessed that when you didn't come into the office. Robert called and he's worried about you."

"You know he hates that name," I comment. Dean's legal first name is Robert, but he's never liked it, so everyone calls him by his middle name.

"I know, which is why I do it," Frank says, forcing a smile.

"Are you here as my friend or my boss?"

"Both, actually. We need to talk."

I step aside to let him in, making my way back to the couch and my food while he closes the door. I reach for the remote to pause my movie and remove the video feed from the screen as Frank takes a seat beside me.

"How much trouble am I in?" I ask.

"Because of Robert? None now that he's been terminated for dereliction of duty, but I wish you told me you were seeing him."

"Why? So you could demote me?"

"Not if you confided in me as a friend, Olivia. I can separate being your boss and your friend when the occasion calls for it."

"Well, I can't. All I see is the detective who came to my house when I was six to tell me my mother was dead. I don't see you as a friend, Frank, only as a boss."

"You used to come to me when you were younger and things began to become harder for you and your dad."

"That was then, but it all changed when you dropped me off at the academy."

"It was the right place for you to go. Being a detective is who you were meant to be. You told me that's all you ever wanted to do, and you wanted to do it to make your mother proud."

I bite my lip as I work on choking back tears. "Why are you here, Frank? And don't give me a bullshit answer."

"I'm reassigning the Marsh case to Foster."

"What? Why?" I ask, dumbfounded.

"Hayden's team recovered semen matching your father's DNA in the victim's apartment. When the connection between you and the sample were made Hayden called me immediately. I can't let you work this case if your dad's involved."

"You can't be serious?"

"I'm very serious. I can't have you handling it because you might have a biased view on what you find or discover. It would put the whole case in jeopardy."

"You think my father's a suspect? That man can't even kill a fly let alone cut someone's throat."

"Is that your opinion or fact?" Frank asks, turning serious.

"Fact."

"I'm sorry, Liv, but I can't let you be a part of this investigation."

"God damn it," I utter. "This is ridiculous. Have Foster handle everything related to my dad, but let me work the rest."

"The chief is making the call on this one, not me. He'll never go for what you're proposing. My hands are tied."

"I don't believe this shit."

"It's just one case, Olivia. You've already been placed back into rotation to get assigned the next one."

"I don't give a damn about the next one. I want to work this one."

"Why?"

"Because it's my job."

Frank studies me very carefully. "There's more to it than that."

"No there isn't," I reply, lying. "If my father did it, then I'll arrest him like I would any other criminal. Why are you trying to make something out of nothing?"

"Because it's not nothing, Olivia. This case could open up some old wounds for you that have never properly healed. When was the last time you saw your psychiatrist?"

"What the hell does that have to do with anything?" I blurt out as I abruptly stand.

"You need to talk to her to prepare yourself in case your father is named a suspect in the young woman's death."

"This is insane. I don't need therapy for something that hasn't happened yet."

"I'm ordering you to do this, as your boss." His face reddens with anger as he stands. "As of now you're on paid leave until after this case is either solved or I get a clear bill of health from your psychiatrist."

"Don't do that," I plead. "I haven't done anything wrong."

"See a therapist, then I'll let you work, but not this case."

Frank storms out of the house, slamming the door shut behind him while I stand awestruck by the sudden turn of events, baffled at everything that just transpired. I need to vent my rage, so I go into my bedroom to dump everything out of my bag. I put my CSB credentials in the back pocket of my jeans with my wallet and return to the closet where I keep my gun case and ammunition. When I'm back in the living room I lock the gun in its case, place it in the bag along with a box of ammunition, secure the bag to my back, and head into the garage, leaving my cell phone behind so I'm not bothered by anyone. I put on my helmet and ride my motorcycle, my destination being the Gardens sector. Normally I would go to CSB headquarters and use their gun range, but as I've been put on administrative leave for the moment I decide to go to Foxtail Park, which is a public range.

I travel through Hunnat passing the CSB building and turn right when I reach the intersection of Lange and Birch. Crossing into the Gardens sector is like civilization comes to a sudden end. It's nothing but forest and wildlife preserves, gardens, lakes, and is the largest sector in Asmor. There isn't any housing in the Gardens, not even a CSB outpost or gas station. It'll take me a good hour to reach Foxtail

Park, which is a drive I don't mind making. Tall pine trees line the road as it bends with one of the many lakes that fill the land. The air is crisp and fresh, which is a far cry from the rest of the state. I could stay here all day and probably will.

The turnoff for the park comes upon me quickly, so my tires skid over the gravel when I make a fast right. It's another ten minutes before I reach the gun range, the lot sparsely filled with cars. Parking my bike, I remove my helmet, and carry it under my arm as I make my way over to the registration stand. I show the woman behind the counter my credentials so I can shoot for free, but I purchase an extra box of ammunition in case I go through what I brought. She reserves stand eighteen for me, then hands me a pair of shatterproof glasses that I drape around my neck, earplugs, and a roll of targets. I thank her and head in the direction of my stand as the sound of gunfire breaks the tranquility.

I set my things down on the table on the inside of the waist-high fence that separates my stand from the others. I'm the only shooter down at this end of the range, which makes me very happy. I unroll the targets, taking one to the end of the field where I tack it to the board, then return to my stand and check the magazine in the clip as well as making sure I have a bullet in the chamber. Before I start firing, I put the earplugs in and secure the glasses to the bridge of my nose. I take a deep breath, and as I exhale I shoot, hitting the target dead center. I don't stop until the magazine is empty. When I turn around to add more rounds Dean is standing there with his arms crossed over his chest. I glower at him as I remove the earplugs and sit down on the bench to refill the magazine.

"What are you doing here?" I ask, incensed by his intrusion.

"I wanted to talk to you about last night," he replies, shoving his hands in his pockets.

"How did you know I was here?"

"Because this is where you always go to get away from the world. You're a creature of habit, Liv, especially when you're angry or stressed. Please, can we talk?"

"There's nothing to discuss. Joe banned you for life from the club, he's making me work the floor Friday night wearing that asinine

42

bikini, and it's all your fault. Oh, and thank you so much for calling Frank. You nearly got me fired."

"I only did it because you wouldn't talk to me. I knew you wouldn't turn him away."

"Why does that matter so much to you? It's not like we're a couple."

He doesn't respond, but instead looks down at the ground, avoiding eye contact.

"No, Dean," I say, securing the full magazine back into the clip, loading a bullet in the chamber. "I don't do relationships and you know that. You said it yourself the other day… we're fuck buddies, nothing more." I set the gun down, take another target, and secure it to the board over the one I just used. Dean is still standing their looking sheepish when I return to the table. "We've had this discussion before."

"And I'm always hoping you'll change your mind."

"We're both too damaged to make this work. It's better to leave things the way they are. Besides, I'm sure I'm not the only woman you've got a thing for or are sleeping with," I say, trying to hide my emotions as they work their way to the surface. I feel if I can keep him at a distance, then he can't hurt or disappoint me like other men have.

"Sure, I've fucked other women, but you're the only one who's managed to get under my skin." He steps into the stand, placing his hands on my arms. "I need you, Olivia. Please don't shut me out."

Sighing, I lift my head up to the sky feeling as if I don't have a choice in this matter, but it's not anything Dean is saying, it's my own pathetic need to be wanted. "You're not moving in with me."

"Not yet," he says, smiling.

"God, Frank may be right. I need therapy."

"When did he tell you that?"

"This afternoon when he came to check on me because of your call. He's placed me on paid leave until I see my psychiatrist."

"Why the hell did he do that?" Dean asks, becoming furious.

43

"I'd rather not talk about it." I pull away, mentally retreating into a shell I've built for myself over the years. "What are you going to do for work? I heard you got fired this morning."

"The owner of Ataxia offered me a job as head of security, so I took it before the axe fell at CSB. I'll be making double what I did as an officer and that's not including bonuses and tips I can earn."

"I hate that place," I grumble.

Ataxia sits in the heart of Nok, a few blocks east of Verdigris. It's the largest arena in the sector and hosts weekly fights between trained boxers and amateurs. Not to mention the mud wrestling, mixed martial arts, and cage matches that happen there as well. It's where grown men go to relieve their pent-up testosterone by watching others beat their opponent until they're good and bloody or unconscious, and drool over women pulling each other's hair out and ripping the string bikinis from their bodies in vats of mud while another woman hoses them down afterward in front of the panting and horny men. Many who wind up at the clubs where escorts are provided—Verdigris being one of them.

"Maybe I can get you to compete in one of their matches," he says, wrapping his arms around my waist as he starts nuzzling my neck.

"You don't have enough money to get me to do that. And besides, you get jealous if another guy looks at me like last night."

"Growsky smacked you on the ass and wanted to see you naked," Dean says, his anger returning.

I shiver at the memory and pull out of Dean's grasp. "I want to forget last night ever happened." I retrieve my gun from the table. "I need to be alone right now."

"What the hell happened after I left?" he asks, seizing my arm, turning me to face him since I had my back to him.

"Don't worry about it, just go."

"Liv, what aren't you telling me?"

"Leave, Dean," I say, becoming upset.

"Fine, but we're not done discussing this. Call me when you get home."

He kisses me, then leaves, but the rage I was feeling earlier which brought me to the gun range has now changed to depression and I want nothing more than to crawl into bed and hide. I take my time cleaning up my spent shell casings, taking down the targets, and locking the gun in its case. After securing everything in my bag, I toss out the earplugs, return the glasses and unused targets to the woman behind the counter, and head home. When I turn onto my street there's an unfamiliar car parked in my driveway, so I go around the bend in the road to enter through the rear garage door. I place the helmet on its hook while the door closes, then set my bag down on my desk as the doorbell begins to ring. I glance at the small screen and the face that appears is one I haven't seen in years. She's a little older and her long, light brown hair has the occasional silver streak to it, but other than that she looks exactly the same as she did the first time I met her.

"Fuck," I mumble, unlocking the door. "Frank called you, didn't he?" I ask my visitor.

"It's nice to see you, too, Olivia. Can I come in?" Dr. Beverly Randall asks, a cloth bag in her hand.

"And if I say no?"

"Then I'll let Frank know you're being difficult, which will only prolong your leave from CSB."

"I haven't had dinner yet."

"Good thing I brought Chinese," she says, holding up the bag.

I step aside to let her in, then close the door behind her. She goes into the kitchen since she's been in my house before, though it's been a while. As she's heating up the food in the microwave I set out plates, utensils, and glasses on the small dining table by the patio door. I grab a cold beer from the fridge and offer her one, but she turns it down. When the food is ready, we sit across from each other and fill our plates with brown rice and orange chicken. Bev gets herself some water before she starts eating.

"I don't need a psychiatrist," I begin the conversation.

"Frank thinks you do, and so do I," Bev says. "It's been years since I last saw you and everyone can use a little help and a friendly ear."

"And anything I tell you will go straight to Frank."

"You know that's not true. I swore an oath that I'd never divulge anything my patients tell me, no matter who asks." She takes a sip before continuing. "Frank told me about the case he removed you from. Do you know why he did that?"

"Of course I do," I snap. "Don't you?"

"Yes, but I want to hear your opinion on the decision."

"It's bullshit," I say, my voice rising as my temper takes control. "I don't give a damn my father might be involved. It doesn't matter what happens to him."

"Why do you say that?"

"Because the guy is a pathetic loser. He means nothing to me."

"You didn't use to think that way. What changed?"

"I grew up," I retort.

"I think there's more to it than that. You just don't want to admit it because then it would make your fears real."

"I'm not afraid of anything," I utter, almost growling.

"How long has your mom been gone? A little over twenty years, isn't it? Her case has never been solved, right?"

"What does that have to do with this?"

"Your dad was a suspect in her death just like he is in this case."

"He had an alibi."

"Staying home with a sick, sleeping six-year-old isn't much of an alibi. Especially when neighbors recall seeing him leave the house a few hours before your mother's body was discovered. There's no telling what he was doing during that time."

"CSB cleared him. His microchip showed he was home with me at the time of her death."

"But it was suspected those records had been altered. After all, he worked in the Hub and had access to its recordings. He had the means and the knowledge to manipulate the information."

"He didn't do it!" I shout. "And he didn't kill this bitch either."

"Are you sure?" Bev asks, goading me. "From what I've seen of the crime scene photos the two were killed in the same manner, posed the same way, and dumped in similar locations."

"I've never seen my mother's crime scene photos, so how would I know that? It's just a coincidence," I grumble. "I thought you came here to help me, not antagonize me."

"I am here to help you, but I need you to admit what you're fearing."

"Fine!" I yell. "I'm scared that my father killed my mother and now this girl. All right? Does that make everything better?" The realization of what I just said hits me and I feel cold inside. I set my fork down, shoving my plate away. "Why did you force me to say that?"

"Because it's something you've been hiding from yourself for years. Now, maybe, we can finally start working on your issues and you can go back to work."

"You make it sound so easy, but that's going to take months if not years, and I can't be unemployed for that length of time."

"Frank will assign you a new case when this one is solved."

"That can still last months and years. Foster doesn't have a good track record at closing cases."

"True, but Frank is helping him on this one because of how similar it is to your mother's."

"I still say the two aren't related."

"Hopefully they aren't and your father can be cleared in this one as well."

We finish eating, clean the dishes, and Bev places the leftovers in her bag, but she doesn't leave just yet. We sit in the living room where I turn on the television, but keep the volume low.

"Are you still seeing Dean?" she asks.

"Unfortunately," I mumble. "He nearly got me fired from Verdigris yesterday."

She gives me a quizzical look, so I tell her what happened at the club. Every. Sickening. Detail.

"And Dean doesn't know?"

"He'll kill Glen and Joe if he finds out."

"But you're still going to work at Verdigris?" she asks, puzzled.

"How else am I going to make any money now that I'm not working?"

"You're on paid leave, Olivia. There's no reason to degrade yourself any more than you already do."

"Then I'd be stuck living in Berrin and I won't be able to keep my car and motorcycle. I'd rather go through the torment and make the money, than lose what I want most in life."

"Possessions don't make people happy."

"No, but they sure do numb the pain."

"Ever thought of settling down and having a family?"

"You know I can't."

"Yes, you can. Having your tubes tied is reversible. I'm still perplexed why you did it at such a young age."

I was sixteen when I made the decision to never have kids. While my father was in a drunken stupor, I had him sign a form giving his permission to have the procedure done. Of course he had no idea what he was signing. He still doesn't know to this day about it and I'm never going to tell him. Dean and Bev are the only ones who know, not even Frank is aware. There's a lot of things only those two are aware about, like the tattoos I have, including the red angel wings on my back between my shoulder blades and the exploding star on my hip. The lily on my right ankle is the only one visible to the world. The next ink I get will be hidden from all—except maybe Dean.

"No kid needs to live in my fucked-up world. It would make being a detective harder."

"As well as the promiscuity with working in Nok."

"I don't sleep around," I counter. "Joe would never put me in that situation."

"He did last night."

"No, that was Dean's fault. If he hadn't showed up none of that would've happened."

"There's probably some truth to that."

The doorbell rings, causing the video feed to pop up in the corner of the television showing a very nervous Dean pacing the porch.

"Well, speak of the devil," Bev comments. "Go and let the man in, Olivia. It's obvious he wants to see you."

"You know he's bad for me, right?"

"Yes, but he's also someone I feel you need in your life right now."

"You're going to regret those words." Standing, I head over to the front door.

"Probably," she snickers.

I barely have the door open when Dean barrels his way inside.

"I told you to call me when you got home," he utters, livid, then his face falls when he notices I have company. "Dr. Randall. I didn't realize that was your car outside."

"Olivia and I had a dinner date, but it's getting late so I must get going," she says, then takes her bag and goes to the door. "It was good seeing you, Olivia. I'll call on you Thursday."

"Why was she here?" Dean asks the moment the door is closed.

"She already told you," I reply, taking the laptop off the coffee table and placing it back on my desk to charge.

"You haven't seen or spoken to Bev in years, and the two of you just suddenly decide to have a dinner date? I'm not buying it, Liv."

"Why can't you ever leave anything alone?"

"Does her being here have anything to do with you being placed on leave?" he asks, worry and distress covering his face.

"I didn't do anything wrong, so don't look at me like I'm a wounded animal."

"Then tell me what's going on?" He's obviously growing frustrated. "Why is it so hard for you to open up to me?"

I lower my head, place my hand over my closed eyes, and try to calm myself down before answering. "I'm not doing this. I've had a long day and just want to go to bed."

He grabs my arm as I turn away. "Not until we talk."

"Let go of me, Dean," I say in an even tone to mask my ire.

"No, Liv. I need to know what's going on with you."

He's not going to drop this until I give him what he wants, but in the same breath I'm terrified to tell him as it would make my fears a reality like Bev said it could. Confessing to her is one thing, but divulging my pain to Dean is something else altogether. "The chief took me off the homicide case I was assigned yesterday. Frank gave it to Foster to handle."

"Why would the chief do that?" Dean asks, perplexed.

"My father was involved with the victim and he's on their short list of suspects," I answer. "And apparently there are similarities between this case and my mother's, so until this one is solved I'm on leave."

"Liv, I'm sorry," Dean murmurs, pulling me into his arms.

I linger in his hold for a while, relishing his musky scent. "Can you make sure the doors are locked and set the alarm while I get ready for bed?" I ask, then tell him the new code.

He doesn't inquire why I changed it in the first place, and I'm glad as that would just lead to another fight.

While he's doing that I turn my cell phone back on, making sure to delete all the messages, both voice and text, that Dean left. His were the only calls I missed, but I do have a few new emails, one of them being from Richard Cassidy's secretary. She's provided me Brooke's personal details, her cell number, and a list of known associates. I lock the phone's screen before replacing it on its charger, then head into the bathroom to brush my teeth and use the facilities. Dean enters the bedroom carrying a bag, which he must have had in his car.

"Seriously?" I gripe.

"It's just a few things, Liv. Not my entire apartment."

He goes into the bathroom while I strip down to nothing as I prefer to sleep naked even when I don't have company over. After getting under the covers, I turn off the light on the nightstand. It's not long until Dean is lying beside me, his naked body pressed firmly against mine, his erect cock poking me in the back as I lie on my side. He rolls me over, his lips finding mine.

"Are you always turned on?" I ask, my pulse quickening.

"Only around you."

I spread my legs, bending my knees to allow him entry. His mouth moves from my lips to my neck, then my breasts. I dig my nails into his back as he thrusts himself inside me, which causes him to moan. Pushing my hands above my head, he holds them in place as his mouth devours mine. He lets me shift my weight, so I can pin him to the bed. With his hands on my hips, he has me take over the speed. He hollers when I drive him fast, but just before he climaxes I slow down, prolonging his agony. His fingers find my clitoris and he massages it, getting me nice and wet. I close my eyes as I fuck him harder and faster until I orgasm, seizing him in a hold that causes him to come. Bending over, I kiss him heavily, which makes us start all over again. It's close to midnight when we finally tire and fall asleep.

Four

"Hey," Dean says, shaking me. "Luke just called. He wants me to come in early today to go over security plans for the big fight he's hosting Saturday night."

"Who's Luke?" I ask, not quite fully awake.

"Luke Cobb, the owner of Ataxia."

My eyes fly open at the sound of his name since he's also the owner of Club Deviant and Lesley's boss, but I try to conceal my excitement. This may be a chance for me to interview the man without Frank knowing I'm butting into the case.

"What kind of fight?"

"It's a special bout between the two top boxers in the country. Luke has been trying to host this for months and now has the backing to make it happen. The winner takes home a million dollars. Luke is anticipating the arena will be packed, so if you're working at the club that night expect it to be extremely busy." Dean leans over and kisses me hard. "I'll see you later, babe."

As soon as I hear the front door close I get out of bed, putting on my robe, which I keep hanging on the bathroom door. I go sit at my desk, turning the laptop on since it had shut itself off during the night, as well as checking my phone for messages, which I have none. I test my access to the CSB mainframe, hoping Frank only blocked me from the Marsh case and not the entire network. Thankfully, I can still access everything, just nothing pertaining to that particular victim. I open the email from Richard's secretary, then copy the cell phone number she provided for Brooke into one of the databases to run a scan for its location and activity. While that's going, I search the small list of friends Brooke is known to hang out with and all have criminal records for drug possession, identity tampering, or theft. I'm surprised by the type of people she's associated with considering she doesn't have any arrests of her own, but that could easily have been deleted if her father paid the right amount of money to the correct people. I guess even rich girls need to rebel every once in a while.

The secretary provided me Brooke's date of birth, so I create a partial serial number and send it to my contact at the Hub to pull recordings on Brooke's whereabouts. I'll wait to see what results I receive before contacting any of her friends out of fear they may tip her off that her father is looking for her. That's if she's hiding voluntarily.

I get into the shower, dress, then take the bag with the locked gun case and box of ammunition into the garage where I set it down on the workbench which divides the garage in half. After turning on some music from the stereo panel embedded in the wall by the door into the house, I remove the gun and disassemble it. I'm very meticulous and anal about making sure my weapons are cleaned after every use. I've known officers who had their lives cut short because of misfires or jams from poor maintenance. Once every part is clean, I put the gun back together and take the box of ammunition I purchased from the range, placing it in the gun safe that stands behind the workbench. I have several weapons stored in here, but my CSB issued gun is the only one I ever leave out. No need to advertise the type of fire power I have on hand.

Leaving the case on the workbench, I take my gun into the house, setting it down on my desk while I check to see if any results have come back on Brooke's cellphone. It's currently not hitting any towers, so it's either off or dead. The last call received is from Richard, and the last call made is to someone named Riddle. That has to be a club name since many of those who frequent the seedier areas of Nok use aliases when working or selling to hide their true identities. Unfortunately, none of the CSB databases contain club names, so I add this person's number to the system and begin a trace on it. As I make my way to the kitchen to get something to eat my cell phone begins to ring, so I have to backtrack to my desk to pick it up. I notice I have a couple of missed calls as Joe's name flashes on the screen.

"Yes, Joe," I say after selecting the audio option.

"I need you to work the next four nights starting tomorrow," he says, a little out of breath.

"Let me guess, you heard about the fight Luke Cobb is putting on Saturday at Ataxia."

"How do you know about that?" he asks, stunned.

"Dean told me. He works for Cobb now that he's been fired from CSB."

"Huh. I wonder how long that's going to last," Joe says, chuckling. "Well, I need you as people have already begun rolling into Nok from all over the place, so every bar and club will be packed before, during, and after the fight. And I'm not going to buy any shit ass excuse that you're working a case because I know you've been put on leave."

"I hate that you know people," I grumble. "Am I wearing that god-awful outfit all four nights or just Friday?"

"Friday only, and I suggest you shave, otherwise those tiny little hairs will get caught in the snaps whether you decide to open them or not."

I shiver at the idea as well as the implication. "You're despicable," I retort.

"You'll thank me after the money you'll earn this weekend," he says, then hangs up.

I roll my eyes, then look at the calls I missed. One is from Frank, but he didn't leave a message, and the other three are from my father, which doesn't surprise me. I ignore his voicemails, deleting them before calling Frank.

"Has your dad been trying to reach you?" he asks the moment he answers.

"Yes, but I haven't spoken to him and I've deleted the messages he left."

"Good." Frank lets out a sigh. "Don't be surprised if he tries to come to your house. Foster questioned him last night without me being present like I told him I wanted to be, and now your dad's upset and agitated."

"God damn it, Frank. This is exactly why you should've left me on the case," I practically shout. "You know how my father can get when being questioned by officers if you or I aren't around to circumvent his behavior."

"I've taken care of Foster's misjudgment, but I want in no way for you to speak with your dad at all. If he comes around call me"

"What, exactly, did Foster say to him to set him off?"

"I'd rather have that conversation with you in person."

"I'm not coming into headquarters. Meet me at Verdigris in an hour. It's empty except for the cleaning crew and a few bouncers this time of day."

"I'll see you there," he says, then hangs up.

"Fuck!" I scream out of frustration.

I call Joe to let him know I'll be hanging out at the club for the rest of the day and that Frank is meeting me there.

"I'll let security know he's coming, so they'll allow him in."

I grab my laptop, charging port, wallet, credentials, and a couple of notepads and pens, placing them into my satchel before slipping my cell phone into the back pocket of my jeans. I'd forgotten I packed the tablet from the office into the bag, so I remove it, setting it on the desk to deal with later. After securing my gun on my waistband, I make sure all the doors are locked, then head into the garage, setting my bag down on the passenger seat of the Nimbus. Once I'm on the street, I set my alarm as the door closes and head toward Nok. I should tell Dean where I am in case he comes back to the house while I'm still away, but he's the least of my worries at the moment. There's no telling what my father will do now that he knows Lesley is dead and God only knows what else Foster said to him. His drinking will more than likely increase even after all his efforts to get it under control. Frank and I are the only ones he trusts. Me because I'm his only child, and Frank as he was the detective in charge of my mother's murder, which is now classified as a cold case, and he cleared my father as a suspect. Though with what Bev said last night it doesn't seem to be the consensus of the rest at CSB. He'll never be fully exonerated until the killer is caught—I just pray it isn't him.

Parking my car in the alley behind the club, I grab my bag, and punch in the code to unlock the backdoor as it's non-business hours. As I reach the floor the bright lights are on and the smell of sanitizer fills the air like heavy perfume. I take a seat at the bar, setting out my laptop and notepads so I can continue searching for Brooke. The two bouncers charged with daytime security come by to greet me as they would've seen me enter from the cameras at the backdoor. I go behind the counter, pouring myself some water and filling a bowl of peanuts.

The cell number for Riddle comes back to a young man named Carter Byrne. Adding his name to my list, I pull up his information. He has a record of drug charges along with stolen property convictions, assault and battery offenses, and a pending indictment for sexual assault against a minor. I search his name under SVU's records to obtain an address for him and I'm not overly surprised it's in Roscow Apartments, and in the same building Lesley lived, only a floor below. I look for another location associated with him and come across the address for the Requiem, an underground club next to Temptation's former location. I'll wait to see what the Hub comes up with before I dare step foot into that deviant den.

"Olivia, Frank's here," one of the bouncers calls to me, standing by the main entrance.

"Let him in."

I close my laptop so Frank doesn't see me working as he comes down the steps to reach the club floor. I go behind the counter and pour him a soda, which I set in front of the stool next to mine, then retake my seat.

"What shit did Foster stir up?" I ask.

"He brought up your mother's murder when he was discussing the Marsh case and the similarities between the two," Frank replies. "It sent your dad into a tailspin. He began raving about his innocence in both cases, that he'd never hurt anyone he cared about, how it's all been a misunderstanding. I have Randy keeping an eye out for him, but he hasn't been back to his apartment since Foster pulled him into questioning. He didn't show up for work either, and he's already on a thin line with his bosses at the plant."

"How did he react when he heard about Lesley's death?"

"He was overly distraught, which bothers me. The last time I saw him this rattled was when your mom died."

"Did Foster ask why he was with someone like her?" I'm furious with the idea of the two of them together.

"Your dad claims he was lonely and they began hooking up after he started going to Club Deviant on his nights off. I have Aleese's team keeping an eye on his movements for me."

Aleese Richards is the CSB contact at the Hub. Her team is designated solely for the homicide squad, but she helps me out with favors, which I pay her for under the table. "Do you know where he is right now?"

Frank takes out his cell phone from his coat pocket, pulling up a text message from Aleese. "At the moment he's a block from your house, so it was smart for you to come here. You may want to find someplace to crash for at least the next few days until he calms down. There's no telling what he might put you through in this agitated state."

"Why can't you just pick him up and hold him in the detention center if he's such a danger to himself and me?"

"Because he hasn't committed a crime, Liv. Just because he's going through a rough time isn't a reason to hold him in a cell. See if Joe will let you stay here until things blow over."

"I've got a great security system at home, so I'll be fine," I reply, purposefully forgetting to mention Dean. "I know the results came back on Lesley's chip because I was about to look at it when you knocked on my door yesterday. Were you able to determine where she was killed?"

"No," he answers, his cheeks reddening slightly. "I had Aleese run the serial number again just to make sure the results she sent were accurate. I can tell you where Lesley was a few hours before her death, but nothing until her body was found in the convenience store parking lot."

"Was she killed at the club?" I ask, perplexed.

"Security footage shows her leaving just after three Sunday morning and heading toward one of the rail stations, but she disappears before she even makes it to the train."

"That's not possible."

"Her chip stopped recording her movements from the time she left the club until we received the call."

"How? The only people with access to override a microchip's function work in the Hub. Did any of them have a connection to the victim?"

"Not that we're aware of. Aleese is conducting an internal audit on their systems to ensure their integrity."

A lump begins to form in the pit of my stomach. "Where was my father during this time?"

"At Club Deviant until three when it closed, and just like Lesley's chip, his goes offline for several hours. But unlike hers it starts recording again around six a.m. Sunday where Lesley's didn't restart until one am Monday."

"My dad doesn't have access to any of the equipment at the Hub like he used to, and those he knew while working there have all retired or refuse to speak to him." Then a thought strikes me. "I need to check something."

Opening my laptop, I enter my passcode to get to the main scree where I review my emails, hoping Aleese has sent me something on Brooke's chip.

"What are you doing?' Frank asks.

"I'm working a case for Joe and needed to have a serial number searched, so I'm checking to see if Aleese sent me the results."

"What case, Olivia?" Frank asks, sounding incensed.

"It's a missing person," I reply. "You know I do shit like this on the side."

"It doesn't mean I approve of you breaking CSB's rules and regulations," he says, glowering at me.

I roll my eyes as I look through Aleese's email, then play the recording of Brooke's chip through the CSB program that translates the information into a timeline, mapping out the person's movements for the last three years before it's recycled as the data can't be stored forever and there's over thirty million people in Asmor to monitor. Once the information is done compiling, I notice Brooke is currently at the Requiem and there's a gap in time between three a.m. and six a.m. Sunday morning.

"Looks like it was a system failure," I say, pointing out the discrepancy.

Frank calls Aleese, telling her to run all chips belonging to CSB officials to see if the error recorded was widespread. It's going to take her days to obtain the information, but she's going to make it a priority.

"Who hired you?" Frank asks after putting his phone away, then raising his glass to his lips.

"Richard Cassidy. His daughter, Brooke, is missing."

Frank nearly spits out the soda. "Fuck, Liv. You do realize who he is, right?"

"I know my history, Frank. It was drilled into us at the academy."

Richard Cassidy's father is the man who invented the tracking system the government uses to monitor its citizens. The street running along CSB headquarters is named after him as well as many of the buildings in our nation's capital.

"Let SVU handle this," Frank says, panic filling his eyes.

"Richard hired me. If he wanted CSB involved, then he would've gone to them directly. Why are you so worried?"

"Because a man like Richard Cassidy could destroy your reputation as a detective if you fail him."

"I'll be fine, Frank."

"Let me know if it becomes too much for you as the family can be very demanding."

"Sure," I say to pacify him.

He leaves, a sense of dread lingering in his place. After cleaning up our glasses, I put my laptop and notepad away before heading out to my car where I sit and debate what to do. I need to go home and change if I'm to go to the Requiem tonight, but then I'd be setting myself up for my father to come and bother me. The clock on the dashboard reads 5:05 p.m., and the club doesn't open until midnight. I also don't know what time Dean will be back, and seeing as he hasn't called me he's probably still at Ataxia. My cell phone begins to vibrate, but I don't recognize the number on the display so I let it go to voicemail. The phone beeps, letting me know a message was left, so I listen to it.

"Hello, Ms. Darrow. This is Kane Cassidy. My father spoke to me about you, and I was wondering if you were available to discuss more about the situation regarding my sister. Please give me a call back at your earliest convenience."

I return his call, which he picks up on the first ring.

"Are you free for dinner?" he asks after the normal introductions.

"Yes, I can meet you somewhere. I'm currently in Nok."

"How about Glasshouse in Crer? It's on Wright just on the other side of Hunnat. Say in about a half hour?"

"I'll see you then."

After I get off the phone I quickly look up to see what the attire is for Glasshouse as I've never been inside of it before. It's casual so I should be fine in my jeans, black sweater, and boots. I lock my gun and credentials in the center console of the car, and tuck my wallet into the back pocket of my jeans before turning the car on and slipping it into gear. I should reach the restaurant with barely a few minutes to spare if traffic is on my side, but given it's rush hour I highly doubt it.

Reaching the restaurant around 6:15 p.m., I decide to use their valet parking as I've kept Kane waiting long enough. I hand the keys to the attendant, receiving a chip in return, which I put in my front pocket. Normally I'd carry some sort of handbag, but I wasn't prepared to go out this evening. Glasshouse is in the shape of an octagon with floor-to-ceiling windows and a dark gray brick façade, the roof coming to a slight point in the center. Outdoor seating flanks both sides of the entrance, the tables filled with diners as tall heaters burn to stave off the encroaching coolness of the evening. I step into the entryway where lounges line the outer edges as a hostess station takes up much of the room, a partition blocking the waiting area from the rest of the restaurant. The interior of the building is white with silver accents. Off to the left is a bar with lit cabinets displaying bottles of alcohol and decorative pieces.

I know this is a casual environment, but I begin to feel underdressed and significantly out of place. Only a few of the patrons are wearing jeans while the rest are in business suits or dresses. I start to second guess this meeting when a young woman carrying a menu approaches me from the hostess station.

"Ms. Darrow?" she asks, unsure if she's addressing the correct person.

"Yes."

"Mr. Cassidy is waiting for you," she says, relaxing. "Follow me please."

We pass through the partition, going to the right and around dozens of crowded tables. I notice in the center of the room is a waiter station where drinks are filled and utensils secured into nicely trimmed bundles along with various monitors where orders are currently being placed and sent to the kitchen staff in the back. I'm shown to a table on the far right against one of the windows. A tall man with a firm athletic body, short, blond hair, and only a slight resemblance to Richard Cassidy stands as I approach. Kane is wearing dark dress pants, a pressed shirt with a tie, and a jacket.

"It's a pleasure to meet you," he says, extending his hand for me to shake before I sit.

The hostess hands me the menu, then scampers off as a busboy comes along to fill one of my glasses with water.

"I'm glad you could meet me on such short notice."

"I would've been here sooner, but traffic was horrible," I say, becoming nervous as Kane looks at me with hypnotizing blue eyes.

I'm not getting the same uncomfortable feeling I had when I was around his father, but then again I'm not nearly naked.

"Your reputation precedes you, Ms. Darrow."

"Please, call me Olivia," I say, my face flushing ever so slightly.

"My father has quite a few friends whom you've helped, and they highly recommend your services. Have you been able to find anything on my sister?"

"As a matter of fact, I have," I reply, just as the waitress comes over to take our order. I have to quickly look through the menu to decide what I want, which is a simple chicken Caesar salad and a glass of white wine. I wait for her to leave before continuing. "From what I found she might be hiding at a club called Requiem. I was planning on going there tonight."

"That's an underground club, isn't it?"

"Have you been there?" I ask, looking at him quizzically as only a few outside of the club scene know that. I hadn't pegged Kane as a partier, but you can never tell about people.

"A few times," he says, blushing. "In my younger days, that is. I haven't been there since my father appointed me CFO of his company ten years ago."

"You were awfully young to take on such a prestigious role."

"I'm smarter than most men twice my age," he says, his arrogance beginning to show, which turns me off rather quickly. "It was the easiest business decision my father ever made, besides hiring you, of course."

I smile to hide my detest as our drinks arrive. While Kane nearly swallows his in one swig, I nurse mine mainly because I'm not a fan of wine, but it seemed like the appropriate thing to order. He gets up to obtain another drink directly from the bar, leaving me alone. I'll be glad when I can bring Brooke back to her haughty family, wiping my hands clean of them, like I do with many of my Waterside clients. When Kane returns he's not only carrying a new drink for himself, but another wine for me. I thank him as I set the glass down next to the one I've barely consumed.

"Tell me, Olivia, what got you into detective work? I would've assumed a beautiful woman like yourself might have easily chosen another profession."

"It's personal," I reply, taking a drink.

"Everything we do in our lives is for personal reasons," he says, leaning forward. "Did you join CSB because of what happened to your mother?"

"You've done your research."

"Of course. It would only make sense for me to know who my father is entrusting with the safety of my sister. I can't have just anyone nosing their way into our family. Is your mother's murder the reason you went to the academy?"

"As I said, Mr. Cassidy, it's personal. And I wouldn't consider myself nosing into your family as I'm simply looking for Brooke, not skeletons in the family attic."

"I'm sorry," Kane says, aware of my change in attitude. "I've always been overly blunt my whole life. It's one of my flaws that I've been trying to work on. I didn't mean to upset you."

"Perhaps dinner wasn't such a good idea," I say, starting to stand when Kane reaches out, grasping my arm.

"No, please, Olivia. Stay. I'm behaving rather rudely. This isn't how I wanted our first meeting to go."

He appears genuinely upset with himself, so I sit back down just as our entrees arrive. At this point I simply want to eat my meal and leave, but it's clear Kane isn't ready to call it a night as he orders dessert and we haven't even begun eating yet. We make small talk, mainly about his father's company and my work as a homicide detective. There isn't much he doesn't already know about me, which bothers me, but I try not to let it show.

"Are you single?" he asks as our plates are cleared and coffee poured.

"It's complicated."

"It's a yes or no question," he says, chuckling.

"Are you?" I ask in return.

"Yes, at the moment. It's hard for someone like me to find a woman to date as they're always interested in only the money I possess and not me as a person."

"I have a friend, but I don't consider us dating. He's more like the occasional roommate."

"Is it serious between you two?"

"No. At least, not on my end. I know he wants more, but I don't—not from him, anyway."

"Why is that?" Kane asks, clearly interested.

"He's more than I'm willing to handle," I reply, being honest.

"I'm sure you can handle a lot," Kane says, smiling.

Dessert arrives, but it doesn't quiet the conversation.

"How do you know Joe Ambrose?" Kane asks.

"I work for him at Verdigris as a bartender and sometimes a waitress."

"Really?" Kane looks surprised, nearly choking on his food. "I can't picture someone like you working in a place like that."

"It supplements my income so I'm not trapped living in Berrin."

"I'll have to stop by some night while you're working."

"Why? To see me in one if the lovely outfits Joe makes us wear?" I ask, teasing him.

"What other reason would there be?" He winks, then his mood changes. "Is that where you were when my father met with you?"

"Unfortunately," I reply, trying to hide the shiver that wants to rattle my body.

"Figures. Richard will do anything to see a young woman scantily dressed. Even pay them good money for the brief encounter."

"Won't you be doing the exact same thing if you came by the club?"

"I'd be there to see you, not your clothing. Besides, I'm not in my late fifties trying to hit on twenty-something's or younger. I swear that man has no scruples."

"He's not the first one I've encountered who acts or thinks with only one appendage, and I doubt he'll be the last." I choose not to use my normal vulgarity as I'm not sure if Kane would find it funny or crude.

"If only his cock were as big as his ego," Kane says, laughing, which causes me to as well. "What time do you plan on going to the Requiem tonight?"

"It doesn't open until midnight, so somewhere around there."

"Want any company?"

"No. Especially since I don't know the nature of why your sister is staying there. If it's voluntary she may act out or run if she sees you."

He nods. "Then I'll wait until I hear from you."

The waitress comes over, so Kane pays for our meal, then he walks me out. I hand my chip over to one of the valet attendants while Kane does the same. My car pulls up to the curb. I hand the young man several dollars on top of what I owe him for the service. Kane stares at my car as I swing the door up.

"A Nimbus. That's a pretty expensive sports car. Are you sure you only bartend and waitress at Verdigris?"

"Well, I also extort men who live on Waterside," I reply, winking. "I'll let you know what comes of tonight."

I close the door, pulling away just as Kane's car arrives. I head home, but barely get a block from my house when I spot my father's car idling in front of my neighbor's home down the street. I loop around and return to the club, but before I step inside I call Dean and tell him what's going on—with my dad.

"Are you going to stay at the club?" he asks, concerned.

"For now. What time do you think you'll be back at the house?"

"Not until late. I'll call you when I'm leaving and we can deal with the asshole together if he steps foot on the porch."

I hang up, leave my bag on the seat and my gun locked in the console, then head inside. Joe's in his office with the escorts even though not all are working tonight, so I linger off to the side while he has a meeting with them about the fight and how he expects the next several nights to be extremely busy.

"Because of the amount of money that will be pouring into this sector, let alone Verdigris, you'll be taken home every night by one of the bouncers," Joe says. "I'm not taking any chances with your safety. If you'd prefer to stay here, you can spend the night in one of the vacant apartments above the club. They're furnished, just devoid of anything personal." He dismisses them before turning his attention toward me. "Is he still there?"

"My father, yes. I'm going to wait for Dean to get off work before heading home."

"I might was well put you on the floor if you're going to stay here for at least the next few hours."

"I actually have someplace to be at midnight, so I was just going to hide in your office until then."

"Where are you going?" Joe asks, narrowing his eyes.

"The Requiem."

"Not dressed like that you aren't," he snaps, scolding me. "Let me catch one of the girls before she goes home. Maybe they can give you something appropriate to wear." He rushes out of the office, returning several minutes later with a young thing named Nikki Burris. I've only seen her a couple of times as she's fairly new. She's my height, thin with large breasts and long, pink hair. "Nikki will take you back to her house so you can go through some of her clothes."

"Are you all right with that?" I ask, as I can't read the expression on her face.

"Sure," she says. "I've been to the Requiem many times, so I know what will work to get you in. Just follow me and I can get you all set."

We leave Joe's office and head into the alley. Nikki drives a little, two-door, red sports car that's parked a few down from me. I get into mine and follow her out of the alley and onto Chestnut taking it to Lange. We pass through Hunnat and into Range, which surprises me. We don't turn until we come upon my street, Clover, where we make a left, then another left onto Tremont when my street comes to an end. We travel down to almost the outskirts of the sector when Nikki makes a right turn onto a driveway of a white stucco villa with a three-car garage. I park in the wide, brick driveway while she enters the garage. After locking my car, I go with her into the house, which is decorated in bright colors and heavily perfumed with lavender.

"Do you live here by yourself?" I ask as we walk through a mudroom before turning right where a crystal chandelier dangles from a two-story foyer.

"Yup," she replies. "Want a tour?"

"Sure."

We move to the left of the foyer, entering a dining room with an attached kitchen that has a scullery, pantry, and the laundry room tucked away behind it. Beyond the dining room is the family room and off that on the right is an alfresco. We go back to the dining room, taking the hallway to the right and enter a small nook where three of the five bedrooms are located. To the right of that is a home theater with leather seats and a floor to ceiling screen. We go back to the front of the house and beside the mudroom is a guest suite. We pass back through the foyer entering the master suite, which has a walk-in closet the size of my living room, a reading room, and bathroom with a shower stall and sunken tub the size of a hot tub.

"How are you able to afford this place?" I ask in awe as we stand in the closet.

"I make over twenty-grand a month working at Verdigris, but I also freelance pulling in nearly a half-million a year."

"What kind of freelancing?" I ask, imagining all sorts of things.

"I'll work parties on Waterside, escort widowers around town or to special events. I even pick up the occasional stripper job at one of the other clubs on my days off, though I don't tell Joe since he has a strict non-compete clause in the contract he makes us all sign." She steps over to the section of her closet where she has various dresses hanging. "What's your bra size?"

"34C."

"I was a 34C before my surgery, so the dresses I have back here should fit you."

"What are you now?" I ask, genuinely curious.

"34 double-D," she replies, and begins pulling out items she thinks will suit me.

I take the pile and am about to go into the bathroom to change when she tells me to do it right there so she can see what works and what doesn't. The dresses are skin-tight, so I have to take everything off just to get them on.

"Nice tats. I love the wings on the back." She scrunches up her face. "We're going to need to wax your pussy," Nikki states, being direct. "All of these have short hems, and men don't want to see the rug you're wearing."

"Do you know how to do that?" I ask, nervous at the idea.

"Sure. I do it all the time," she says, then proceeds to lift up her skirt without hesitation to show me her work. "I'll even go with you tonight as I know several of the bouncers and can get us in for free."

"I guess carrying my gun is out of the question."

"Where would you put it?" she asks, snickering. "I have a small clutch you can use to at least carry your cell phone, driver's license, credit cards, and money. But it won't be big enough for your gun."

I cringe at the thought of entering the club unarmed, but I don't have much choice in the matter. After careful thought, I select a mini dress with spaghetti straps, a zipper that goes all the way down the front beginning at my cleavage, and is platinum in color. Nikki has me try on a couple of high-heeled shoes with thin laces that wind up my legs. At least I can use the heels if I get into trouble since they're long and sharp. She then selects her outfit—a two-piece consisting of a halter top and skirt copper in color with small rivets along the seams—before forcing me into the bathroom where she warms up the wax as she tells me to exfoliate the area. This shouldn't be bothering me as much as it does because of what I've seen happen in the club, but I don't know Nikki all that well and this is certainly an odd way to make a first impression.

I cleanse the area, making sure to dry it completely before I lie down on the tiled floor for her to apply the wax. I've never done this before, so the feeling of hot wax hitting my skin is an odd sensation.

When Dean sees this he may want me to keep it clean for him, but then he'll also ask questions about why I had it done. That's an easy one to answer since Joe suggested I do it for when I wear the bikini. Nikki applies the strips to the wax and we wait.

"I heard you're working the floor Friday," she says to pass the time.

"Yeah, and Joe's having me wear an escort outfit, but in blue."

"Then it's a good thing we're doing this." She takes hold of one of the strips. "How busy do you think the club will actually get?"

"Very." I cringe as she pulls, ripping the strip off like a bandage. "I'm not looking forward to it." She quickly removes the rest, then applies a cooling lotion. "Holy fuck, did that hurt."

"It won't the more often you do it. Just don't let it grow so long. We should do something to your hair was well."

While I cower on the floor, my pussy feeling like it's on fire, Nikki goes through the cabinets under the dual vanity, coming up with a tube of temporary color. I sit on the edge of the tub as she applies it to my hair in streaks, turning my dark blond tresses purple. She hands me a robe, washes her hands, and we head into the kitchen to grab some drinks and a few snacks.

An hour before we decide to leave we go back into the bathroom and wash my hair to remove the excess dye, get dressed, and put on makeup. The tattoo between my shoulder blades shows because of how the back of the dress is cut and I like displaying it whenever I get the chance. Nikki hands me a cloth bag to put my clothes in along with a clutch in the same color as the dress. I place what I can inside, shoving the rest into the bag. When I'm outside, I take the bag with my laptop and place it in the trunk along with the bag Nikki loaned me. I wait for her to back out of the garage, then follow her out the way we came.

As I pass my house I spot my father nervously pacing in my yard, unsteady on his feet. His clothes are disheveled, his hair sticking up in places, and his car idling along the curb. He won't know it's me as I drive by as he doesn't know I own the Nimbus, only the motorcycle. I fight the urge to veer the car in his direction and continue down Clover to Lange where I turn right and put him behind me.

Five

After entering Nok, Nikki turns left onto Devon several blocks
later and parks in a lot across the street from a row of clubs close to
the sector's border with Berrin. As I get out of my car I notice
Temptation right next door to the Requiem, it's windows and doors
boarded up as its once pulsating sign dangles along the front of the
building. The entrance into Requiem is a simple door with a flashing
neon sign cascading down the glass, changing colors every few
seconds. Music escapes into the night when Nikki opens the door,
and we descend as the club sits under a couple of tattoo parlors and
smoke dens along with parts of Temptation. At the bottom is a line
to get inside, so the two of us wait like everyone else going through
identity checks, though theirs isn't as sophisticated as the more
established clubs.

"Nikki," one of the bouncers says, wrapping her in his thick, dark
arms. "It's been a while."

"I finally have a night off," she replies. "How packed is it?"

"Not as much as it should be, but it's still early. Why don't you
and your friend head inside?" he says, lifting the velvet rope blocking
our entry.

Nikki kisses the bouncer on the cheek and shoves me inside,
right onto the dancefloor that's wall-to-wall people. Lights flash
down from the ceiling; strobes illuminate the corners as a DJ booth
sits at the far end between two doorways. Nikki takes my hand and
we begin to make our way through the crowd as I continuously scan
the room for Brooke. I made sure to put a copy of her photo on my
phone so I can wave it around if I get the opportunity. Nikki takes
me down a hallway off the back-right corner of the room that leads
to a bar, which isn't as busy as the dance floor. We take a seat along a
counter against the far wall, placing our orders on touchscreens
adhered to the horrid paneling. I glance around the room, looking for
emergency exits, and begin to panic when I don't see any.

"Is the main entrance the only way in and out of this place?" I
ask as our drinks are delivered, Nikki paying for both.

"Yes."

"That's against the law," I say, my CSB persona taking over.

"Relax, Olivia. This place is riddled with sprinklers," she says, pointing to the ceiling.

One of the classes I took at the academy was fire safety and prevention. We studied how fires can spread through buildings if given the proper ventilation and fuel supply. The cheap décor, the lacquer-covered wood, the overstuffed furnishings, and wall paneling would be enough to gut this place in minutes, killing everyone inside regardless of the sprinklers. If the fire load is too big, no amount of water suppression inside the building will contain it. I need to find Brooke and get her out of here as fast as possible.

"I'm going over to the smoke den. Do you want to come?" Nikki asks, pulling me out of my paranoia as she points to a hallway opposite the bar, not the one we came in from.

"I'm good here," I respond, my anxiety growing with each passing second.

"Then I'll catch up with you in a bit."

She grabs her drink, slides down from the stool, and disappears into the growing crowd. I take a deep breath, letting it out slowly to calm myself as I absorb every face around me, praying one of them belongs to Brooke, but none do. With my drink in hand, I wander over to a hallway that's dimly lit, this one leading deeper into the club and into a lounge with a long sectional that wraps around the room, a coffee table in the center that has what appears to be remnants of a fine white powder covering much of its surface, but I doubt it's dust. I move onto the next room, which is identical to the one I just left, then head to the only other doorway leading out, finding myself eventually in the smoke den Nikki had mentioned. Five hookahs rest on the floor, each with pillows around them for people to sit while inhaling. I spot Nikki at one, flirting with the young man next to her, so I proceed down another brightly lit hallway and into a second bar. Turning, I head down the hallway on the right only I'm cut off by a locked door, so I go back to the bar. I find two other doorways—one leading to an office, and the other goes right back to the dance floor.

The club is a labyrinth with only one way out. I begin to feel claustrophobic as the pulsating lights start to give me a headache and the urge to run grows. I feel a hand on my back, which causes me to tighten my grip on the glass in my hand, ready to throw it in the face of whomever is about to bother me.

"Red angel wings? I never would've thought you were that kind of woman," Kane says, after I turn around. "The purple in the hair is a nice touch."

"What the hell are you doing here?" I ask, noticing he's in the same clothes he wore at dinner. "I told you not to come."

"I wanted to see you again," he replies, smiling as he looks me up and down. "You look amazing. Do you have any other tattoos?"

"Two. A lily on the inside of my right ankle and an exploding star on my right hip." I down my drink.

"Maybe I'll get to see them. Come with me." He wraps his arm around my waist, escorting me back to the first bar. We sit along the wall where I reorder my drink, but Kane doesn't order anything. "What do you think about the place?" he asks, leaning close to me to be heard.

"It's horrid."

"This isn't even the worst of them," he says, laughing, paying for my drink when it arrives. "There's one a block away that is several stories below ground, each level offering a different option of entertainment and debauchery. The walls are thin, the lighting harsh, and the music terrible. Not to mention they water down the drinks and charge double for what it would normally cost. Have you had a look around?"

"Briefly. Just enough to get a lay of the land. There's only one room that's locked, so I'm guessing Brooke might be in there."

"Do you know how you're going to get inside to find out?"

"I'm working on that," I reply, finishing my drink.

"Let me help you." He proceeds to remove the glass from my hand and leads me back to the dance floor where he wraps his arms around me as the music thumps in my ears

73

"How, exactly, is this helping?"

He spins me around so my back is against him, but his arms still around my waist while his head rests on my shoulder. "How about now?"

From our vantage point on the floor I have an unobstructed view of the hallway leading to the office. It's an entry point I hadn't noticed before as I'd returned to the dance floor previously from the far end of the room by the DJ booth. This particular doorway is close to the entrance, but was blocked by the bouncer when Nikki and I entered. We stand in the corner as several men come and go from the office, one of them being Riddle, who I recognize from his mugshot. Kane spins me back around so I'm facing him.

"Did that help?" he asks, leaning his forehead against mine.

"For the moment," I reply, my pulse quickening the longer he holds me. "I need a drink."

Pulling away from Kane, I make my way back to the bar. He joins me, only this time we sit on one of the couches. I have to carefully cross my legs, so I don't expose myself. Kane orders a drink for me, along with one for himself, then pays for them when they're delivered. He rests his arm along the back of the loveseat, his fingers brushing my bare shoulder.

"You seem nervous," he says. "I hope it's not because of the company."

"No, not at all. I hate being in places that are overly cramped and crowded. Verdigris can get busy, but it's never made me feel confined like this place does."

"What would help you relax?"

"Finding your sister and getting the hell out of here."

"I'm sure there's another way." Kane removes my glass, setting it down on the end table behind him along with his own drink.

His lips meet mine and heat encapsulates us instantly. It doesn't take long for his hand to start playing with the zipper of the mini dress, dragging it down, but not too far. His mouth moves to my neck, and I close my eyes picturing what his skin will feel like against mine. He kisses me deeply, our tongues battling for dominance. He stops, pulls me from the couch, and takes me down the hallway that leads to one of the lounges, but he doesn't stop there. We come to a halt in the dimly lit corridor that connects the two lounges, which are still empty. His mouth takes mine as his hands lift the hem of my dress, his fingers slipping inside of me as I drop the clutch to the floor. I moan at his touch, my fingers grappling with his pants. The moment they hit the floor Kane enters me and I gasp. He presses me against the wall, thrusting himself as hard as he can, causing me to become wet within seconds.

"Oh God, Olivia," he moans in my ear.

"Don't stop," I counter.

He comes, but he doesn't stop until I orgasm. I have to bite my tongue to keep myself from shouting his name as every nerve ending vibrates with pleasure. He kisses me hard, our hearts racing as the heat builds again. He has me wrap my legs around his waist as we continue to fuck, sweat soaking our bodies. My orgasm hits first and doesn't let up. Kane buries his head in my shoulder as he moans, his legs trembling as he comes. He holds me against the wall while we try to catch our breath, then I bring down my legs so I'm standing on my heels. Kane fixes his pants as I adjust my dress, cleaning myself off as best I can, but it's not long before his hands are all over me again.

"We need to find your sister," I utter as he plunges the zipper on my dress, taking my tit in his mouth.

"I know," he mutters. "But I just can't help myself with you."

"There you are," Nikki says, interrupting us.

I quickly zip up the dress as Kane ducks behind me, mainly to cover up the bulge in his pants.

"Sorry," she says, blushing. "I'll come back."

"No, it's fine, Nikki." I grab her arm. "What is it?"

"Riddle is looking for you," she says, startling me.

"What?"

"Oh, sorry, Olivia, not you. He wants to speak with Mr. Cassidy. He's waiting for you in his office."

"Did he say what he wanted?" Kane asks, puzzled by the request.

"Riddle says he knows why you're here," she replies. "That's all he told me to convey."

"Do you want me to come with you?" I ask, fearing the worst for some unknown reason as I pick the clutch off the floor.

"Yes," he replies without hesitation.

Nikki makes her way back to the smoke den while Kane and I head to the entrance for the office off the dance floor. The guard at the door opens it upon our approach, then closes it once we've entered the dank room. Smoke stains from old cigarettes piled on rusting ashtrays have turned what was probably once white walls into a yellowish-brown. Riddle is standing against a broken metal desk, his heavily tatted arms crossing his chest, a scowl creasing his face while two guards wait for orders as they stand by the other door that leads to the second bar.

"It's about fucking time," he hisses, a foreign accent escaping his mouth, which I wasn't expecting. "That cunt you call a sister has been refusing to leave my establishment for the past two weeks and has snorted everything I have inhouse. Get her the fuck out of here."

"You could've saved us the trouble of tracking her down and just told us she was here," Kane says, angry.

"The bitch wouldn't let me."

"I highly doubt she was in any condition to give demands," I say.

Riddle scrunches up his face, narrowing his eyes. "Who the fuck are you?"

"A friend," Kane replies for me. "If you want Brooke gone so badly, then bring her here and I'll take her home."

"Not yet." Riddle waves his finger as he moves around to the other side of the desk, plopping his skinny ass down on a cracked leather chair. "She owes me money."

"How much?" Kane asks, glaring at the poor excuse for a human being.

"Forty grand."

"That can't all be for drugs," I retort.

"No, dearie, it's not," he says, leering at me. "There's also alcohol and other services she needs to pay for. I don't give anything away for free."

"I don't have that amount in cash on me," Kane says. "It'll take me a day or two to obtain."

"I sincerely doubt that." Riddle crosses his feet on top of the desk. "Rich fucks like you always have ample amounts of money lying around. Go get it."

Kane reaches out to take my hand, but freezes when he notices the gun one of the guards is holding, aimed in my direction.

"She stays. And you can add another ten grand for her release as well."

"What?" I ask, astonished. "I'll call CSB."

"Good luck with that," Riddle scoffs. "Cell phones don't work down here, and if lover boy goes to the cops he'll find your corpse alongside his sister's."

"I'm not leaving without Olivia."

"Then I guess you're not leaving at all."

"Go," I say to Kane. "I'll be fine."

"No."

I kiss Kane, then rub my finger over the chip under his skin. "Trust me."

"If anything happens to her I'll burn this place down with you and your patrons inside," Kane says, seething, then leaves as the guard on the other side opens the door.

I'm forced to sit on a couch in the corner of the room, crossing my legs at the ankles to protect my modesty while the guard continues to aim his weapon at me.

"I know you," Riddle says after a few minutes of tense silence. "You work with Nikki at Verdigris."

"How could you possibly know that?"

"I make it a point to know my competition, especially one as arrogant as Joe Ambrose."

"I hardly call you a competitor with this rundown firetrap. Everyone in Asmor knows the clubs that line the outer limits of Nok are all run by measly little rats who don't know their ass from a hole in the ground."

Riddle nods. The guard without the gun comes over and backhands me across the face, cutting my cheek with the heavy jeweled ring on his finger.

"Whores like yourself should be more respectful of their owners," Riddle says.

"You don't own me... no one does."

"I will when your boyfriend doesn't return with my money. He's going to leave his sister here to rot just like he will with you, and when he does you're mine for the keeping. Joe won't be able to afford the price I'll place on your head to secure your freedom. Cunts like you are replaceable. Especially to men like him."

I set the clutch aside, lean over, and begin unlacing the heels. "Since we're going to be here for a while, I might as well get comfortable," I say, slipping the shoes off, but I don't let go of them. "These hooker shoes are killing my feet."

Riddle smiles as the zipper on my dress slides down a bit, without any help from me, since I'm still leaning over. My breasts press against the material, causing them to bulge and the zipper to fall down even farther. I should fix the dress, but then I think about how to use this to my advantage. I lean back, uncrossing my legs to allow my dress to hike up a little, but I still hold onto the heels. Riddle licks his lips, then stands and makes his way over to me.

"Did you enjoy fucking your lover in my hallway?" he asks, sitting beside me, his putrid cologne invading my nostrils.

"You saw that?" I ask, feigning embarrassment.

"I see everything that goes on here." Riddle strokes my arm. "Like most clubs, I have cameras hidden everywhere."

"But I don't see any security monitors, so how did you notice us?"

He reaches into his back pocket, removing his cell phone and begins scrolling through the images as they appear on the screen.

"I thought cell phones don't work down here?" I ask as he shows me a live feed of the smoke den.

"Only mine does as I use signal boosting equipment located on the roof of the building that's programmed strictly to my device."

That doesn't surprise me, and I'm thankful that the tracking program used in the microchips is powerful enough to penetrate walls and solid ground, which is how Aleese was able to find Brooke—and how I'll hopefully get out of this situation.

"Now, Olivia, I need you to tell me something." Riddle puts away his phone, then leans close to me, his hot breath hitting my face. "How did Kane finally realize where his sister was?"

"You'd have to ask him," I reply. "I was simply invited along for the night."

"But you came in with Nikki, not Kane."

"He told us to meet him here. I can't help it we arrived first."

Riddle studies me very carefully, making me nervous the longer he remains silent. He places a hand on my thigh as the other reaches for the zipper. "I wonder how good a fuck you really are. Kane seemed to enjoy it and he always has great taste in women."

Before Riddle can move the zipper farther down, I swing my shoe, hitting him in the side of the head with the heel. Blood runs down his face, but as he goes to retaliate I slam the heel into his face, embedding it into his cheek. He shrieks from the pain, and I throw the other shoe at the guard with the gun, knocking the weapon out of his hand. The two dive for me as I slip between them, grabbing the weapon and firing it into the wall behind the couch. Both of the doors into the office fly open, Frank spilling into the room along with several officers.

"Jesus Christ, Frank. It took you long enough," I quip as the officers place Riddle's guards under arrest and call for a medic to tend to Riddle's wounds while those in the club are starting to be questioned by CSB detectives from SVU.

"How'd you know I was coming?" he asks, out of breath.

"Because you're overprotective of me," I say, getting to my feet, handing him the guard's weapon. "I knew the minute I told you who I was working for you'd start trailing me, or at least have Aleese trace my microchip. Where's Kane?"

"He's waiting for you in the hallway."

"And Brooke?"

"She was found in a locked room off one of the bars. She's being looked at by medics and will more than likely be going to the hospital."

Grabbing my clutch, I leave the one good shoe behind before making my way into the hallway. Kane holds onto me tight, his body trembling, but I can't tell if it's from worry or adrenaline. His lips find mine and it takes everything for us not to fuck each other in the middle of the club.

"Don't ever do that again," he says, as if scolding me.

"I was fine, Kane. I knew what I was doing."

"Your face is cut. Did Riddle hit you?" Kane asks, becoming enraged.

"It was one of the bouncers, but I'm fine. I'm more than able to take care of myself. Besides, I knew Frank was going to get here. He'd never let anything bad happen to me."

Kane continues to kiss me, only stopping when the medics bring out Brooke. She's extremely thin, heavily bruised, and her lips and skin are dry to the point of almost cracking. Her body shakes as she grips tightly onto a blanket wrapped around her shoulders. She smiles when she sees Kane, but it disappears when she notices me, his arms still wrapped around my waist. Her eyes continue to linger on us as she makes her way across the dance floor.

"We're taking her to Grove Hospital in Vale," one of the medics says while his partner helps Brooke up the stairs. "You should follow us."

Kane looks at me, sorrow heavy on his face.

"Go," I say. "She needs you."

"I'll call you after she's settled," he says, then kisses me again before following the medic up the stairs.

Turning, I notice Frank standing behind me, his face contorted in a grimace. "Dean is going to kill you," he says.

"Only if you tell him."

"Yeah, right," he says, smirking before his tone turns serious. "Just be careful, Liv. You know what Dean is capable of when he's jealous. Make sure you're doing what's right for you in the long run and not simply in the moment before things go too far with Kane Cassidy." He pats me on the arm. "Go home. I've got this handled."

I head up the stairs, the streets lined with squad cars, their lights flashing, cutting into the din of the night. When I'm seated in my car, I lock the doors and let out a deep breath as I start to shake mainly from the feelings that are coming over me about Kane. I'll need to calm down before I get on the road, but my angst rises when my cell phone rings, Dean's name rolling across the screen. I select the audio feature as I'm not ready for him to see me in this rattled condition.

"I've been trying to get a hold of you for hours," he snaps. "Where the fuck are you?"

"I'm on my way home now," I say, exhausted. "I just need to settle my nerves for a few minutes."

"What the hell for?"

I tell him about the missing persons case I was hired for, leaving out the details about who hired me as it's none of his business. I divulge very little except I do mention Nikki and Riddle, then lie where I need so the scenario fits the story.

"Why didn't you have me go with you?" Dean raves. "I could've helped you before it escalated. At least Frank was there, but what if he wasn't?"

"Look, I'm tired and I just want to go to bed when I get home. If you're going to be an asshole when I get there, then leave. I don't need any more stressful shit tonight."

I end the call, toss the keys into their holder, and head back to Range. Dean's car is sitting outside as I pull into the garage, my father nowhere in sight. I finally notice the time; a few minutes after three. I leave everything in the car as I don't want to deal with it at the moment, then drag myself into the house after setting the alarm. Dean is sitting on the edge of the bed when I enter, his arms folded over his puffed-out chest as his already red face darkens.

"Fuck off," I utter as I make my way into the bathroom before he can open his mouth. I stand in front of the vanity removing wipes to clean the makeup from my face.

"Where are your shoes?" he asks, leaning against the doorframe.

"I left one in Riddle's office while the other is embedded in his face," I reply, ignoring the disdain oozing from his pores.

"Is that one of Nikki's dresses?"

"I already told you it was on the phone."

"Did you have one of the medics take a look at the cut on your cheek?"

"No, as it's just a scratch."

"Tonight could've ended quite differently if it wasn't for Frank."

"Yes, Dean, I know. Look, I just want to get washed up and go to bed. Go home if you're going to be a pain in my ass." I unzip the dress, letting it fall to the floor. I catch Dean's face in the mirror, his mouth gaping open.

"When did you do that?" he asks, pointing to the area between my legs.

"Tonight," I reply, brushing my teeth. "Nikki did it since Joe is having me wear the bikini on Friday. She said it'll be easier if I'm clean shaven because of the snaps in the crotch."

Dean saunters over and waits until I'm done before grabbing me around the waist, pulling my head back against his chest with his other hand. "That'll make things so much easier," he whispers.

The arm around my waist drops between my legs, forcing them open. His fingers find my clitoris with ease, and I come in a matter of minutes, soaking the tile floor. Dean doesn't wait to get me into bed,

82

S.L. Waters

but lowers me onto the wet floor, strips, and fucks me until the sun rises. I hurt everywhere as I crawl into bed, Dean collapsing beside me.

"You're cleaning the bathroom," I mutter as I begin to doze off, but his snoring tells me he's already asleep.

When I wake Dean's gone, but he left a note on the pillow telling me he went into work. I check the time on the clock on my nightstand and am surprised it's only eleven. I step into the bathroom to take a shower, noticing the floor has been scrubbed, and I smile as I was certain he hadn't heard me. I try to wash the purple from my hair, but it simply lightens instead of coming out. Once I'm dried and dressed, I retrieve my things from the car, setting the bag with my laptop down on the desk along with my gun and credentials while taking the bag with my clothes and clutch into the bedroom. I have to do a load of laundry for tonight, so I gather the fishnet mini dress and matching thong along with other items, tossing them into the washer. I'll need to have Nikki's dress dry-cleaned before returning it to her. As I'm making myself lunch, I check my phone, noticing I have dozens of missed calls from my dad, but no messages. Kane hasn't called, which makes me feel both relief and sadness. I need to consider what happened last night between us a blip on the radar and move on.

Taking my sandwich into the living room, I turn on the television, and start a movie, but it's quickly interrupted by pounding, my security camera displaying my father battering my door. I mute the movie hoping he didn't hear it in the first place, and try to ignore his pleas.

"God damn it, Olivia!" he screams. "Open the fucking door! I need to talk to you! I know you're home, so open the God damn door!"

I reach into my pocket for my cell phone and call Frank, placing him on video so I can show him what's happening.

"I'll be right over," he says. "Don't answer."

"I wasn't planning on it," I utter.

83

The minutes tick by like hours, the pounding relentless. I'm surprised my neighbors haven't called the CSB station, but many of them are either at work or don't give a shit what happens down the street as long as it's not on their front porch. Something outside catches my dad's attention and causes him to bolt to his car. His tires squeal when he drives away just as Frank's sedan pulls into the driveway. He steps onto the porch, enters the code that I gave to him after changing it, and the alarm system disarms. I don't have to get up to unlock the door since he has a key, so he lets himself in, locking the door behind him.

"I thought I told you not to stay here," he utters, sitting beside me.

"Where am I going to go? I refuse to be chased out of my house by some drunken asshole."

"I hate to say it, but maybe stay with Dean. Your dad doesn't know him, so there's no chance of him finding you."

"Dean's not going to go for it. He's practically moved in here." I gesture around the living room.

When I came home last night, I noticed more of his crap in my garage and a few boxes stacked in the corner of the living room. I was too tired to confront him about it, but I'll need to do it soon before everything he owns is here. I don't think there's much more that he has to bring over.

"You can stay with me."

"No way. Your tiny home is barely big enough to hold you."

"It's not that small," he says, pretending to pout. "What about the apartments Joe has above the club?"

"Dean's been banned from Verdigris, and I sincerely doubt he'll want me staying there by myself."

"You're just full of excuses, aren't you?"

"Has Foster made any headway on the case?" I ask, ignoring his remark.

"At the moment he's talking to everyone who slept with the victim based on the DNA we found in her apartment. Most of them have alibis even with the Hub being down for those three hours."

"Has Aleese determined what happened?"

"Not yet."

"What about Lesley's friends and coworkers? Have you found her cell phone?"

"We haven't been able to track down anything she had on her person or was carrying that night. The records we pulled only show calls to her boss, your dad, and a handful of acquaintances, all of which are being questioned or have already been cleared. We're slowly making our way through the list of her friends we've been able to gather as well as her coworkers."

"How about her breast implants? Did you discover who paid for those?"

"Her boss did."

"Have you questioned him yet?"

"No. He's been hard to get ahold of lately. Both Foster and I have left numerous messages for him, but he hasn't returned our calls. Anything else you want to know?"

"Have you tracked down the person who reported her body?"

"You're not going to believe this, but the number logged doesn't exist, and the security cameras outside of the convenience store short out for a few minutes. One moment the parking lot is empty, and the next her body is there on full display."

"It has to be someone with a technological background."

"Like your dad?"

"No," I snap.

"Liv, he has the degree and the knowledge to manipulate security systems, cameras, and the like."

"Don't you think if he really did anything like what you're suggesting he would've simply broken into my house and not banged on the door? Are you actually looking at anyone else or just him?"

"We're going over everything, Olivia, but your dad keeps rising to the surface. The only reason he hasn't been arrested yet is because everything we have is circumstantial."

"I…I can't deal with this," I utter, getting to my feet after setting my uneaten sandwich on the coffee table.

"When do you see Bev again?"

"Um, today, but I don't know what time she's coming over."

"Go pack and I'll take you to the club."

"I have laundry I need to finish, then I'll drive myself over."

"I'm going to place a patrol car outside just in case your dad decides to return. Call me the minute you leave and when you reach Verdigris. I'll see if Bev can come over now."

He leaves as I go to throw my things into the dryer, then head into the bedroom to pack. I send Joe a text message telling him what's happening, but I hold off on informing Dean because I know how he's going to react and I just can't deal with his anger right at the moment. I make sure to add towels, toilet paper, and toiletries to my bags as I sincerely doubt the apartments have any of the essentials. When the dryer dings, I put my outfit for the club in the bag on top of the one I'm going to have to wear tomorrow. I double check what I have, grabbing any last-minute items like my laptop, its charging port, my cell phone charger, my credentials, and gun with extra ammunition. I get everything loaded into the Nimbus when my doorbell rings, Dr. Randall standing on my porch.

"Frank said it was urgent I get over here," she says as I close the door behind her. He must have caught her in the middle of a workout since she's wearing tight black leggings, a stained sweatshirt, running shoes, and her light brown hair is tied into a disheveled ponytail. She's also lacking makeup, which is something she never leaves home without donning. "What's going on?"

I tell her about my father's visit, what Frank said about the Marsh case, and I even delve into the details of the night before—including everything about Kane. Bev takes a seat on the couch as I pace, her expression hard to decipher.

"Well, first, I think it's smart for you to stay elsewhere until either your dad is cleared or charged," she begins. "It was stupid of you to have gone to the Requiem without proper backup or protection, and I'm not just talking about your gun. You're playing with fire having unprotected sex, especially with someone like Kane Cassidy. He's had countless girlfriends over the years. There's no telling what he might be carrying."

"I'm immunized like everyone else at CSB, and I'm sure Kane has gone through the whole sequence of shots given who he is, so I'm not worried about that."

"That's only if you, and he, keep with the shots on a yearly basis."

"Believe me, I do. It's the one thing I'm very religious about."

"But you sound worried."

"What if Dean finds out?"

"Didn't you think about that beforehand?"

"Yes, sort of. Dean wants more out of this relationship than I do. He's even started moving his shit in here," I say, pointing to the boxes.

"Then tell him to leave."

"I have… in a way. Okay, maybe not in so many words."

"Olivia, take a breath," Bev instructs. "What do you want from Dean?"

"He makes me feel safe."

"Except when he's mad."

"He's never once hurt me," I say, seething at what I feel she's implying. "I don't tolerate shit like that."

"I know you don't, but that's not what I'm saying. Sometimes you do things to push Dean away, like sleeping with Kane Cassidy. Now with you staying at Verdigris it'll be impossible for him to see you, though it's the safest place for you at the moment."

I lean against my desk, my head spinning as the walls begin to press in on me.

"Why did you sleep with Kane?" she asks, after a brief pause.

"Because I wanted to," I reply.

"Are you attracted to him?"

"Yes," I openly admit.

"Have you heard from him since last night?"

"No, but I'm not surprised considering how weak his sister was when we found her. He's more than likely still at the hospital with her or is at home getting some sleep."

"What will you do if you never hear from him again?"

"Move on," I reply. "It's not like I'm in love with the guy. I can move past him and back to Dean. Besides, his father still owes me for the job, so I'll be at least hearing from one of them."

"So in your mind Dean offers security, protection that you've been missing throughout the majority of your life. What does Kane offer?"

"Why does every relationship have to mean something?" I ask, avoiding the question.

"It doesn't always, but given your history it's going to."

I lean my head back, close my eyes, and inhale deeply before responding. "Kane is smart, sexy, handsome. He's the CFO of his father's company."

"Which means he can provide the lifestyle you've been trying to obtain."

"You make it sound like I'm after his money."

"You're not, I know that. I just want you to realize where your choices in men are coming from before you decide to settle down with one of them."

"Why are you so eager to marry me off? God, you sound just like my mother."

"What do you mean by that?" she asks, homing in on the nugget I inadvertently dropped. "Your mother died when you were six. She wouldn't have had conversations like this with you at that age, or did she?"

"Mom always told me not to settle for the first man I slept with like she did. It was her opinion to experience life as fully as possible before being shackled down into a forced existence."

"Did she ever express regret about having you?"

"No. That she always made clear to me… that I was wanted and she loved me more than life itself. It was marrying my dad she regretted. I think if she'd lived long enough they would've divorced."

"Do you know if your dad was aware of how she felt?"

"I doubt it as he was pretty clueless about her needs and emotions. Just like he is about mine. I'm not surprised she had affairs."

"I don't think you've ever mentioned that to me before."

"Frank knows because it came out in his investigation. That's what drove my father to start drinking, even though she was already dead. It tore him apart when her extramarital activities were exploited all over the newspapers and news stations. He couldn't tolerate life anymore and even tried to take his at one point."

"How old were you?"

"Ten," I reply, sitting on the couch beside her. "I'd just come home from school when I found him in the bathroom. Blood was everywhere. I called emergency, then Frank."

"What had your dad done?"

"Slit his wrists. The doctors at the hospital told Frank if I hadn't found him when I did he would've died."

"Perhaps that's another reason why you keep Dean around. You don't want him abandoning you like your father almost did, and if he leaves, whether it's voluntary or not, you'll have a difficult time coping. So you let him run your life because you know it'll keep him close."

"Then what am I doing with Kane?"

"You see in him the life your mother wanted to have and what she taught you to look for even at the young age of six. Being with him is fulfilling some kind of fantasy for you, either real or imagined."

"And if Dean finds out I could lose everything."

"I suggest taking the next several days and contemplating what you want out of your life with these two men. The isolation will be good for you, for once."

"Except I'm working the next three nights."

"Dean can't get to you, and Kane hasn't called you. That's the isolation I'm talking about."

"I hate this," I groan.

"I know. I'll check in with you over the next couple of days by phone as I'm heading out of town."

Bev leaves, so I make sure one more time that I have everything I want, that the doors are locked, and there isn't anything in the garbage or sink since I don't want my house stinking when I return. I get in the Nimbus, call Frank to tell him I'm on my way to the club, and head toward Nok wondering how Dean is going to react when I tell him where I'll be staying.

Six

Joe isn't at the club when I arrive, but there's a key waiting for me dangling from a hook on the inside of the alley door. I get my things out of the car, making several trips up the staircase hidden behind a door beside the storage room. There are two additional floors above the club, each with four apartments. Joe gave me the key to one on the top floor facing the street. I crack open the windows as the cramped space is stuffy and loaded with dust, then spend the next hour cleaning every surface, even stealing supplies and the vacuum from the janitor's closet by the stage on the club floor. I didn't pack any sheets, blankets, or even pillows, so I'll have to see about picking those up before the club opens, which is in six hours as it's just after four.

I unpack what I have, slip my cell phone and wallet into my back pockets, then return to the Nimbus, exiting the alley and heading northwest on Chestnut toward the mall that rests along the river. It takes me a little over an hour to buy what I need because I plan on leaving the items behind when I return home in case I have to crash at the club again. I might as well make it comfortable and get what I like instead of what's on sale. I make a quick stop at the food mart across the street from the mall, purchasing mainly snack items that don't need to be refrigerated. When I'm back at the club I haul everything upstairs, set up the bed, place my food on the kitchen counter, and try to relax a bit before reporting downstairs.

Plopping down on the couch, I wrap my new soft blanket around me as the air has a slight chill, then turn on the television. The stations are few and there isn't anything worthwhile to watch, so I shut it off and pickup my laptop to do a little research on Kane Cassidy. I'm interested in seeing if I can discover anything about the women he's dated. I begin with the society sections of the websites for our local news, coming across only a few mentions of his girlfriends, each with a picture. The women standing beside him have long, dark hair, are overly thin, and wear clothes and jewelry I could never afford. They all smile happily, his arms wrapped around their tiny waists as they pose for the cameras. I try not to compare myself to these girls, but it's hard. I'm a fit and healthy 135 pounds for my five-foot-eight build, yet I feel overweight compared to the women in the photos. I didn't have their upbringing, I don't come from money, and I work hard at everything I do, which is probably something none of them have ever had to deal with in their life.

Scrolling down to the very end of the column, I spot a small article buried beneath it regarding a young woman who's been missing for over a year. It intrigues me, so I check when the article was written, which was four years ago. I study her picture and there's a hint of familiarity to it, but I'm not sure why. I take note of her name before opening the CSB mainframe where I enter in the information from the article to pull up the case file.

Kelly Harris, twenty-three, was last seen arriving at her parents' home where she lived hours after a job interview. She was a recent graduate from Paramount College, which is located in Range only a few blocks from where Kelly lived. She received a bachelor's degree in education and was hoping to teach first grade. Her file contains the recordings for her microchip, which shows her traveling from her interview at an elementary school a few blocks from the university and arriving home just after three in the afternoon, but there isn't anything after that.

Under the case notes the person in charge, SVU Detective Gail Rodgers, states the signal in Kelly's microchip was lost around four while she was still at home. However, when her parents arrived an hour later Kelly wasn't there, but everything else she owned was, such as her purse, cell phone, and car. The phone records show she received one incoming call at eleven that morning, which lasted for several minutes, but the number it came from was blocked and Detective Rodgers wasn't able to obtain any additional information on it, such as a tower location when the call was placed or the type of phone it belongs to, as there are fewer than five brands on the market. Kelly was at home when she received the call, so that doesn't aid in determining who placed it.

Reaching for my phone, I decide to give Gail a call. She answers on the third ring.

"Rodgers."

"Hey, Gail, it's Olivia. Do you have a minute?"

"Sure, Liv. What's on your mind?"

"I was looking over some old cases since I'm bored with being on leave and one of yours caught my eye."

"Which one?"

"Kelly Harris."

"That one still puzzles me," she says, simmering. "How does a woman vanish in the middle of the day from her home? There's nothing to indicate she left the house, yet she was gone when her parents returned from work."

"Could someone have picked her up from the house?"

"Her microchip would've recorded that and it didn't."

"And nothing was found out of place?"

"No. Her parents said nothing had been moved or taken, except Kelly. It's almost like she vanished into thin air."

Then a thought strikes me. "Do you know anything about the case I was pulled from?"

"A little, but not much. You know Foster likes to keep his mouth shut and not share."

I chuckle. "Well, the victim's recordings show a gap in time that can't be accounted for. There's a solid break between three and six a.m. where nothing was recorded, and it looks to have been caused by a system wide failure. Aleese is looking into what might have caused it, but perhaps that's what happened with your case. Did you have your contact at the Hub check for any other discrepancies around the time Kelly disappeared to see if it was more than just her chip?"

"Huh, I hadn't thought of that, but the problem is that data is now gone since it's been five years and the Hub only retains recordings for three."

"Would you mind if I take a look at the case? I need something to do to fill my time."

93

"Sure, that'd be great," Gail says, sounding ecstatic. "Are you free for lunch tomorrow? I can give you the rundown along with the physical file I've been keeping as I don't trust computers to retain everything for as long as we need them to."

"What time?"

"One p.m. here at headquarters up in the café?"

"I'll see you then."

I'm in the process of setting my phone beside me when it begins ringing, Dean's name scrolling across the screen. I select the audio only feature before answering as that's what he's using to call me. If it was a video call his picture would've popped up.

"Hey, babe. I wanted to let you know that I won't be home until Sunday," he says. "Luke is working my ass off with this fight. I'll be staying at the arena until this nightmare is over."

"All right, and just so you know I've temporarily moved into one of the apartments above the club."

"That's probably a smart idea since I can't be around to fend off your dad if he should come calling."

I feel relieved that Dean is okay with the notion of me staying here, and with him at the arena we'll simply be a few blocks from each other, not miles, which surprisingly gives me comfort.

"Hopefully this fucking case will be solved before Sunday as I'm not looking forward to being here any longer than that."

"Don't worry, everything will be fine once the weekend is over. I love you," he says, then promptly ends the call, leaving me stunned by his parting words.

This can't be happening...this can't be happening, I mutter to myself in my head. *No, Dean, don't say that. You're pushing me into a corner I don't want to be in.*

My anxiety skyrockets and I begin to tremble. This is exactly what I didn't want happening and now I find myself in a predicament I don't know how to handle. After setting the laptop and phone on the coffee table in front of me, I head down to the club, making a beeline for the bar, pouring myself some rum, and swallowing it in one shot. I drink two more, so I can numb myself.

"Olivia," Nikki calls from the door leading to the back. "Joe's looking for you. He's in his office."

"Tell him I'll be right there," I say, pouring one last shot.

My head feels a little fuzzy as I make my way to Joe's office, knocking on the door before opening it. He's standing beside his desk, Kane in front of him. The room feels cold and uninviting, and it's being emitted from Kane, which confuses me. I approach the pair cautiously, mainly so neither notice I'm a little unsteady on my feet, then stand beside the two of them, waiting for someone to speak first.

"Kane has the money his father owes you," Joe explains.

Kane holds out a packet of $100 bills equaling $10,000. "Thank you, Ms. Darrow, for your assistance in locating my sister."

"No problem," I reply, hesitating in taking the money.

Kane's demeanor exudes contempt, the arrogance from our dinner very prominent. He scowls at me as if I'm something that should be stepped on and crushed, which hurts.

"I'll be seeing you, Joe," Kane says, then abruptly leaves without giving me a second look.

I stand there frozen with my mouth gaped open. The man I just saw isn't the same one I encountered at the Requiem. I want to think he was acting so formal as a disguise in front of Joe, but I start to feel otherwise. Maybe knowing what his sister was put through has affected him, even though I have no idea what exactly happened to her down in Riddle's cell. I'll need to find out to see if the two are related.

"Olivia, are you all right?" Joe asks, his hand holding onto my arm.

"I'm fine," I reply, lying. "Would you mind keeping this in the safe for me?"

"Of course," he says, taking the money from me. "Have you been drinking?"

"It's been a stressful day."

"Are you going to be able to work tonight?"

"I'll be fine."

I head back to the apartment and munch on some of the food I bought as I haven't really had anything to eat all day and now I've added alcohol into an already tentative system. When it's close to eight I put on the mini dress, apply a bit of makeup, and strap on my heels before heading down. I go through the items we have under the countertop and in the small refrigerators that fill one section under the bar to see what needs to be stocked, then make my way to the storage room. Alice eventually joins me and we start mixing some of the concoctions while the DJ tests his sound system. Nikki sits at the bar in her red getup, a worried expression on her face.

"I was looking for you after CSB raided the club," she says.

"Sorry. I just wanted out of there."

"I heard what happened. That had to have been scary."

"I've been in worse situations."

"You and Kane Cassidy make a hot couple," she says, smiling. "How long have you two been seeing each other?"

"It was the one night. His father hired me to find Brooke, which I did. The jobs over, so we're going our separate ways."

"Yeah, right, Olivia," she says, eyeing me with suspicion. "I saw the way you two were all over each other. Kane is definitely into you. Don't be surprised if he shows up here tonight."

Little does she know he already did and acted as if I was beneath his stature. It would've been better to be ignored, at least then I wouldn't have felt so degraded. Nikki leaves just as the main lights dim and the others come on. It doesn't take long for the club to fill, and I catch word there's a line down the street to gain entry. Joe wasn't kidding about this place being crowded because of the fight, which isn't until Saturday and it's only Thursday. God knows how awful tomorrow night is going to be, let alone the rest of the weekend.

Joe wanders up from the back with Henry beside him. The stool Henry sits on was moved behind the counter before we opened to keep it from being taken, so Alice places it by the partition while I pour him a club soda.

"My beautiful ladies," Henry says, kissing us each on the cheek. "Are you ready for a rollercoaster of a night?"

"We'll do our best," Alice replies.

"Liv, I'm sorry about CSB. I'm sure you'll be back to work there in no time."

"Thanks, Henry."

"Are you good?" Joe asks.

Henry waves him away, pretending to be irritated by the question. Joe chuckles, then disappears into the mass of people hovering around the stage.

The first break we get is right before midnight. I tell Alice to take hers while I keep pouring and mixing drinks. The bouncers have already had their hands full subduing a few men who were getting a little too handsy with the waitresses or were stumbling around from too many drinks. The music is close to a deafening volume making it difficult to hear the orders being requested. I barely hear the man behind me order a rum and Coke, which I make quickly, then turn to hand it to the him only to come face-to-face with my father.

"Fucking hell," I say, dropping to the ground to cover myself. "What are you doing here?"

"I need to talk to you, Livy," he says, his speech slurring.

"Leave me alone. Get the fuck out of here."

"Not until you listen to what I have to say." Raising his voice, he slams his drink on the counter, spilling it.

"Henry, get Joe," I say, panic and fear gripping me. "Dad, you need to leave."

"I'm not going anywhere until we talk," he demands. "Stand up so I can see your face."

"Are you fucking nuts? You know what I'm wearing, and there's no way in hell I want you seeing me in it."

"I didn't kill that girl, Livy. You have to believe me."

"I can't discuss anything about the Marsh case with you, you know that."

"Get off me," my father practically shouts as two bouncers seize him by the arms and begin dragging him away.

When he's no longer in view, I stand up to clean up his mess, but Alice says she'll take care of it as she steps behind the bar. Going into the back, I hide myself in the dressing room for several minutes. I'm rattled and it's taking everything I have to hold off tears that want to spring forth.

"Olivia, are you in here?" Joe asks through the door, which is cracked open.

"Yes."

He enters, a sorrowful expression on his face. "The girls at the door weren't supposed to let him in," he says. "It's been so hectic he must have escaped their notice when they checked his chip."

"Where is he now?"

"In the holding cell begging to see you."

"Did you call Frank?"

"I left him a message, but it's going to take CSB hours to move down these streets. Maybe you should take the opportunity and go talk to him. He can't hurt you behind bars, and you can always leave if it gets too rough." Joe places his arm around my shoulder, pulling me against him in a fatherly fashion. "He's hurting just as much as you are. Take the chance while it's given to you because you may never get it again."

I reach over to one of the chairs in front of the makeup stations, take the robe that's resting there, and wrap it around my body before stepping back onto the floor with Joe closely beside me. We ascend the steps, pass through the main entrance, and turn left where the door to security is situated. Joe enters in a passcode to gain entry, then has me follow him inside the elaborate and spacious room, but has me wait by the monitors while he steps over to the bars for the holding cell to have a word with my father. I can't hear what Joe's saying, but after a brief moment he waves me over as one of the bouncers takes a chair from the corner of the room, setting it next to the cell. I sit, my father mimicking my moves on his side as Joe continues to stand there.

"Behave yourself, Michael," Joe orders. "Don't waste this moment with Olivia. You need to listen to her and she'll listen to you. Be respectful, or my guards will show you a painful way out of my building."

Joe pats me on the shoulder, then leaves. Those in the cell with my dad hang toward the back where the cots are, too drunk or dazed to care what's going on in front of them. I'm having a hard time looking at my father as I like to retain the memory of a fit, athletic, happy man from my childhood, and not the overweight, depressed, and unkempt shell before me.

"I didn't kill her, Livy," he says, his head hanging against his chest.

I want to be a smartass and ask which 'her' he's referring to—Lesley or my mother—but there's a time and place for everything. This has to be about Lesley and his involvement with her. A discussion about my mother will have to wait for another time.

"Why were you seeing her?" I ask, trying to grapple with the idea of the two of them together.

"I was lonely, Olivia. You know what that's like."

"Then buy a damn dog," I snap.

"How can I take care of a dog when I can't even take care of myself?"

"Where did you go after leaving Club Deviant that night?"

"I wandered around for a while to sober myself up enough so I could drive home."

"You could've taken the rail or called a cab. Now there's a gap of time where only you can account for."

"No, the Hub will be able to see where I was and that I wasn't anywhere near Lesley when she was killed."

"Foster didn't tell you about the outage, did he?" I ask, finally raising my gaze to meet his.

"Huh?"

"The Hub's entire system crashed around three that morning and didn't come back online until close to six, leaving three hours no one can account for your whereabouts."

"But I know where I was, isn't that enough?"

"No," I reply, my voice rising. "Did you go near any clubs or bars that would have security cameras along their exteriors? Maybe one of them picked you up and can give you the alibi you desperately need."

He lets out a sigh, his putrid breath hitting me in the face. "I lied to you, Liv. I wasn't wandering around trying to sober myself up. After leaving the club, I followed Lesley for about a block or so before losing sight of her as everything began to spin around. I must have blacked out because I came to in an alley as the sun was rising."

"They're going to arrest you," I say. "You're their only suspect so far."

"Can't you get me out of this?" he asks, begging like a wounded animal.

"No!" I shout, startling those sleeping. "Deal with the mess you made. I'm done."

I begin to stand, but he grabs my arm, gripping me tightly.

"Don't leave me, Livy. I can't... I can't tolerate being alone. I'd never abandon you in your hour of need."

"You did that twenty-one years ago," I retort. "When mom died."

He releases me, tears streaming down his face. I head back to the dressing room to pull myself together, so I can return to the floor. When I'm back behind the bar I mentally shut down, ignoring the chaos around me as I fill glasses, pour beer, and blend drinks. Things start to settle down just after two, which is the time we normally close. It takes another hour for the bouncers to get the building cleared out and all of us are exhausted. Alice sorts through the tip jar dividing the money between the two of us. After taking my cut, I head up to the apartment to crash for the night.

Lying in bed, staring at the drab ceiling, I dare myself to get up. I reach over to the nightstand where I left my cell phone to see what time it is and if I have any missed calls. It's barely ten, and the only call I missed was Frank's around four this morning, so I play the message he left.

"Olivia, your dad's been taken to the men's detention facility to sober up before he's sent back to his apartment. I've filed a restraining order against him barring him from contacting you. He knows the consequences of breaking the order, so this should at least settle things down enough for you to go home. I'll call you later."

I should feel better about being able to return home, but I don't. Everything about the Marsh case bothers me. Hopefully Aleese's team can pinpoint what happened to cause three hours' worth of recordings to disappear. I doubt Foster has located the crime scene yet and that could hold a lot of clues as to who might be responsible. Perhaps retracing Lesley's life is another viable option to determining who might have caused her death. I only remember a few things, such as her previously working at Temptation, but the rest of my notes are all tied up in the case file I no longer have access to... and on the tablet I left at home. I always keep my case notes on there, separate from those housed in the CSB mainframe. I downloaded them before I left the office to speak with Randy the other day.

Tossing the phone onto the bed, I get up to take a shower so I can make a quick run to my house before I meet up with Gail. I have to let the water in the tub run for a few minutes until it comes out clear as it's been a while since the plumbing up here was last used. When I'm dry, I put on a pair of jeans, a black sweatshirt, and my boots before grabbing my wallet, phone, and car keys. I do a quick drive by my house, making sure my father isn't anywhere in sight before pulling into the garage. The tablet is still on my desk where I left it, but dead. It uses the same charger as my cell phone, so I'll have to wait until I'm back at the apartment to gain access to my notes.

I still have plenty of time to kill, but I head over to headquarters anyway as I want to find out what happened after I left the Requiem since I forgot to ask Frank yesterday. I park in the garage, making sure to take the tablet with me so I can charge it at my desk. Before I step onto the elevator, I check to see if Frank is in the office, his name rolls across the screen along with thousands of others. His office is one floor above mine, so I drop the tablet into its port at my workstation, then head up. He's on the phone looking more rumpled than usual when I knock and he signals for me to enter. After closing the door, I take a seat across from him. His dark suit is severely wrinkled, his hair uncombed as he continues to run his fingers through it out of frustration, and the top of his desk is so littered with papers many of them might fall to the floor.

"I don't give a damn how busy he is," Frank snarls, his wide nostrils flaring. "One of his employees was murdered this past weekend and I need him to come in for questioning. It's either here or I send my detectives to Ataxia and make a big scene in front of his promoters… That's what I thought. I'll see him and you in my office at two." Frank tosses his cell phone aside. "God I hate lawyers."

"Luke Cobb giving you trouble?" I ask, leaning back in my seat.

"As usual." He rubs his ruddy face. "You'd think the guy could at least give two seconds of his time to convey some empathy about one of his girls being killed, but no. He has too many other things going on that are more important." Frank drops his sweaty hands on the papers, smearing a few of them. "What can I help you with?"

"I didn't get a chance to ask what happened at the Requiem after I left."

"Not much," he grumbles. "The owner already has a new manager in place just in time for this weekend's fight."

"Carter Byrne doesn't own the club?"

"Are you kidding me, Liv?" He practically snorts. "None of those pieces of shits own the places they run. Requiem is owned by a conglomeration called Centurion. They manage several of the seedier clubs and smoke dens on that side of Nok."

"What's going to happen to Carter?"

"He's down in a holding cell with twenty stitches in his face from your shoe. He's being charged with two counts of unlawful imprisonment. One for Brooke and one for you. He won't be going anywhere for a while."

"How's Brooke doing?"

"The last I heard she's starting to improve. The chief is handling all of that given who the victim is, which is fine by me. Gail told me the two of you are having lunch today." He leans back, plopping his folded hands into this lap.

"She told you?" I ask, surprised.

"She had to get my permission to allow you to see her files. I hope you brought your car as you'll need it to cart all that crap back to your house, or wherever you're staying."

"How many are you talking about?"

"Fifteen."

"For just one missing person?" I ask, astonished.

"No, for five. Each case has three boxes worth of notes and evidence. You shouldn't have volunteered yourself to help the woman out. She has the heaviest case load of any detective in CSB."

"Terrific," I mumble, rolling my eyes.

Frank's smile fades as his tone turns serious. "I heard you spoke with your father last night when he stumbled into Verdigris. Did he say anything to you about the case?"

"Just that he didn't kill Lesley."

"Is that the only thing he mentioned?"

"Yes, Frank," I retort.

"Do you believe him?"

I hesitate in responding, which answers the question.

"Hayden's team is currently processing the clothes your father wore that night. If Lesley's blood is found he'll be arrested and charged with her murder. They're also searching his apartment for evidence."

"And when the clothes come back clean?"

"He'll be temporarily removed as a suspect and we'll continue searching for others."

"Has Foster determined where she was killed?"

"He's still working on that."

I abruptly stand. "Tell him to work harder."

"Olivia, I think there's something you should know," Frank says, which causes me to halt my escape. "Lesley was two months pregnant when she was killed. Lloyd conducted a paternity test on the fetus. The results came back to your dad. Do you know if he was aware?"

"You'd have to ask him," I answer, reaching for the door, slamming it shut behind me.

I return to my workstation, but simply stare at the blank screens in front of me while the world slowly passes by, sickened by the news. I know why Frank told me about Lesley being pregnant. It means my father had a possible motive to kill her… and it's the same one Frank tried to use against my father when they wanted to charge him with my mother's murder. She was pregnant at the time of her death, but it wasn't my dad's child she was carrying. I'm not sure how far along she was as I only heard inklings about it from now former friends of the family. My mother was probably hoping to pass the child off as my father's, but I was too young to know what she was thinking and why she did what she did to our family. My curiosity grows the more her case dwells on my mind, so I turn on my computer and call up her file only to find it's been blocked.

"Shit," I grouse.

I know Frank is the one responsible for my access being denied, which means I'll have to go about obtaining the information another way. I write down the case number to search for the physical file later across the street in the warehouse where old cases, both solved and unsolved, go to die. I'm sure I'll have to go there to obtain Gail's boxes. I'll simply slip a couple of extra ones into my stack. The warehouse is automated, but with heavy surveillance both inside and out. My movements will be tracked along with what I remove from the building, making it a little difficult, but not impossible, to take my mother's files. I check the time on the computer before shutting it down, then make my way up to the breakroom to meet Gail. She's sitting at a table off to the side when I enter. I quickly grab food and join her.

"Glad you could meet me," she says, smiling.

Gail is somewhere in her forties, very curvy, and with short black hair. She's the most analytical person I've ever met—besides Lloyd Rhemick—and she specializes in missing persons for SVU. Her workload far outweighs mine even with an entire branch of the Hub assisting her. It's hard to believe the number of people who vanish while being tracked by the government.

"I saw Frank before I came up. Five cases? Why so many?"

"It was something you said that got me thinking," she says, between bites. "About how there was a disruption in the tracking system from the Hub over the weekend. Kelly Harris' microchip stopped working altogether the day she disappeared. I took the information and applied it to all my open cases, then narrowed down the specs to only those whose chips went completely silent, because as you know if there's an issue or if someone tries to remove a microchip the action gets recorded. I wanted to see what number of open cases I have where the chip simply stopped recording without a known cause documented and I found five."

"You think they're related?" I ask, not quite understanding her reasoning for conducting such a search.

"After the data was compiled, I quickly glanced over a few of the details about each woman and there were several notes that caught my attention. One being they all lived in Range at the time they disappeared, all were in their early twenties, and all were about to start new careers."

"Those could just be coincidental," I utter, trying to mask my sudden unease. "Minute details always blend together. It's the deeper ones you need to ferret out to notice if a pattern exists."

"I know, Liv. It's also a feeling I have. Look them over, and if you don't think they're connected, then shove everything back into their boxes and I'll take them off your hands. You said you wanted something to do while on leave."

"Do you have the case numbers on hand so I can go across the street into storage?"

"I already have the boxes. Frank helped me remove them this morning. They're down in my office. I'll have one of the junior officers help you take them to your car. I also have some of my people at the Hub pulling data from the time frame of the most recent woman who went missing less than a year ago. I'm hoping they find the same gap you discovered in your case."

We make idle chitchat during the rest of the meal, and I sense she wants to discuss the Marsh case, but she bites her lip every time the conversation begins to head in that direction. I want to put Lesley Marsh as far from my mind as possible given the revelation about her pregnancy. I'm utterly disgusted with my father's behavior and want nothing more to do with him. My mind wanders to my mother, causing my hostile mood to deflate into utter despair.

"Olivia, are you all right?" Gail asks, pulling me out of my head.

"I'm fine," I reply.

I finish eating, clean up my tray, and leave. Before I exit the building I make sure to retrieve my tablet from its charger, then head down to the lobby where I wait for the officer. He steps off the elevator several minutes later with two carts filled with brown corrugated boxes, each labeled with the victim's name and case number. I take possession of one of the carts and head over to where my car is parked in the garage. Once everything is loaded, the officer takes the carts back inside while I drive several blocks over to the warehouse, which is located behind headquarters on McCarthy.

The gate for the four-block-wide structure is attached to an electric fence topped with razor wire, and a keypad is the only way to access the grounds. I enter my CSB badge number, allowing the gate to swing open, then shut and lock behind me. Parking close to the building, I input my credentials again onto another keypad to gain access to the warehouse itself. The large, metal doors part and I enter into a vestibule that blocks anyone from physically entering the rest of the way. Only those with proper clearance can get onto the floor itself, which I don't have. The walls surrounding me are made from plexiglass with waist-high doors that open onto conveyor belts that zip along the floor as robotic arms dangle in the air waiting to be awakened.

The panel in front of the wall is what controls the hands, so I enter my mother's case number, ordering them to retrieve the boxes for me, only I'm met with a message.

Evidence boxes for case number 1575398 – Darrow, Nancy were removed by Corro, Frank today at 9:17a.m..

"God damn it," I grumble, then step out of the doors, return to my car, and head back to the apartment above the club.

It takes me several trips to bring everything upstairs. I'm carrying the last box when I run into Nikki stepping out into the hallway from the staircase.

"I didn't know you were moving in," she says, teasing.

"I'm helping SVU with a few of their cases," I explain, juggling the box for emphasis.

"How many since you've brought in quite a few boxes?"

"Five."

"Want any help? There isn't much to do during the downtime."

I'm not sure what to make of the offer, but having additional eyes couldn't hurt. "If you don't mind, that would be great."

"What apartment did Joe give you?"

"The one on the top floor in the righthand corner. Which one are you in?"

"The one below you. I'm sharing it with Alice since there are several of us staying here until the weekend is over, so we're bunched together. She just ran out to pick up a pizza. We'll be up as soon as she returns," Nikki says before departing toward the club floor.

When I'm back in the apartment, I set the box down at the tail end of the group I have lined against the wall, the names and numbers facing outward with several inches between them. I head down to Joe's office for some tape, pads of paper, and pens, then I sit on the floor in front of the first set of boxes, which are Kelly's, and begin the daunting task of assembling the last moments anyone saw Kelly Harris.

Seven

The first thing I pull out is a photo of a lovely young woman with soft features, dazzling blue eyes, and short, blond hair that barely brushes the tops of her ears. Written on the back of the picture are her age, height, and weight at the time of her disappearance. I decide to tape Kelly's photo on the wall several feet above the boxes, then sit on the floor to rifle through the heavy file folders stuffed inside. I'm reviewing the Hub's report on Kelly's microchip when Nikki and Alice enter. Although I already ate, the pizza Alice is carrying smells delicious.

"Shit, Liv. I thought Nikki was kidding," Alice says, setting the grease-laden box down on the kitchen counter. "Is this all for one case?"

"No. There are five different cases here. The detective in charge thinks they're related, which is why she's letting me sift through them all," I respond.

"What are you hoping to find?" Nikki inquires, as she begins to eat.

"Besides these women?" I counter, slightly annoyed by the question. "A reason why they were taken, where they might be, and who could've snatched them."

"How come you're helping this detective?" Alice brings her plate of food over by me, which causes my stomach to rumble.

"It's something to pass the time until I'm reinstated at CSB."

"You got fired?" Alice exclaims, surprised.

"I'm on paid leave for the moment due to a case I was working on. It's a long story I'd rather not go into."

"What do you want us to help you with?"

"Maybe start by going through and seeing if there's a photo of each of the missing women, then taping it onto the wall above their boxes," I reply.

Alice finishes eating, washes her hands in the sink, then starts sorting through the paperwork while Nikki sits on a stool at the countertop. They both offer me some of the pizza as I continue to review the Hub's report, so I stop what I'm doing to eat a few slices, then get back to work. On one of the notepads I write down my findings from the Hub in a quick notation so I can keep it straight in my head when I move onto the crime scene photos. Nothing in Kelly's parents' house was reported as being out of place or missing, except for Kelly. Gail has notes taped to the back of a few of the pictures taken of the house, including Kelly's bedroom, indicating that there wasn't any signs of forced entry, no blood or other bodily fluids were located, and everything was exactly how Kelly's parents left the house when they went to work that morning.

Setting the photos aside, I begin skimming through the interviews conducted, focusing on key questions and answers such as if Kelly was seeing anyone, had she just gotten out of a bad relationship, did she have any enemies, was she on drugs. The consensus among Kelly's parents and friends was she was liked by everyone, had never been in trouble with CSB, didn't do drugs, and was happily engaged at the time she disappeared. Gail did a background check on Kelly's fiancé, but she couldn't find anything significant. Gail had also requested a recording of his microchip for the time Kelly was to have last been seen, but he was out of the state, which shows on the printout.

I glance at Alice, who's making her way through the boxes before I return to mine, pulling a folder filled with data recordings from the Hub showing the location of everyone Kelly knew around the time she vanished. No one was shown as being near her home or even in Range. I next remove an inventory sheet listing everything that was found in her car along with photos documenting how her car appeared when the officers arrived at the house. Empty water bottles lay scattered on the floor in the backseat in addition to an umbrella, fleece blanket, and a first aid kit with the seal still intact. In the center console was a garage door opener, a half-empty box of tissues, a flashlight, a few business cards, a small jewelry box, and an assortment of pens, gum, and mints. Nothing was found under the passenger or driver's seat, and only an air freshener dangled from the rearview mirror.

110

"Whoa," Nikki gasps from her seat. "That's creepy."

"What is?" I ask, as I still have my head buried in the inventory sheet.

"That," she replies.

I glance up to see what she's gesturing toward, then promptly get to my feet and step back from the wall to get a better view of the pictures Alice hung up.

With a quick look, the five women eerily resemble each other, almost like sisters. Hair colors and styles are different, but their facial structures look similar, so I move closer to examine each one. As I go down the line, I flip the pictures up to read the information on their back, noting the age range and residential location for each of them. Gail had mentioned they were all in their early twenties and from Range, but their addresses are nowhere near one another, so that eliminates the disappearances as being a cluster. Each woman was set to start a new job a week after their disappearance, but not in the same field. Kelly was to be a teacher, while another woman was joining a law firm, and another was going to be a medical technician.

"What do you think?" Alice asks.

"They look like they could be related, but there's nothing in their history from what I've been able to read so far to indicate they are," I reply.

"Do you have a photo of their parents?" Nikki asks. "Maybe see if there's a connection there."

Alice sorts through one box while I examine Kelly's before checking the rest, but none have them.

"It was worth a shot," Nikki says, before going back to eating.

I sit down to review the photos of Kelly's bedroom, home, and car once again as Alice and Nikki leave to shower before tonight. Setting the pictures aside, I move onto one of the other cases, hoping to find some connection between them that may not otherwise be obvious. I compare the photos, timelines, Hub recordings, list of friends and acquaintances, places they frequented, but not one thing is the same. I'm sorting through the boxes for case number three when my cell phone rings, Dean's name scrolling across the screen.

"Hey, babe. I was wondering if you could come down to Ataxia for a minute. I have something for Joe from Luke, and seeing as I'm banned from the club I can't deliver it like I'm supposed to," he says.

I look at the time and it's just after six. "Sure. I can be there shortly."

"I'll have one of my guys let you in."

I hang up, slip the phone in my back pocket, and head out. The streets are starting to gain traffic, both vehicular and pedestrian, which isn't unusual for Nok, but it is for the time of day. I can only imagine what tomorrow is going to be like and I'm not looking forward to it. I wait until I'm down by the massive arena before crossing the street since it's on the other side of Chestnut. Large screens are affixed to the exterior, each one touting the fight while holographic images of the fighters rise from projectors lining the roof, adding to the already obnoxious signs that make up the scenery. Stepping up to the main entrance, I knock on the glass to get the guard's attention. He unlocks the door to let me in, then tells me to head down the hallway on my right as Dean is in the security office.

The interior of Ataxia is nothing but concrete, glass, and blue-painted steel where the exterior is nearly all chrome. The hallway bends to the left as the arena is oval-shaped, and I find the entrance for the security office on the right past a set of elevators. The door is cracked open, so I knock before pushing it aside. My heart stops when I notice Kane standing beside Dean; the two hunched over a desk going through paperwork. I try not to show my unease as I step into the room.

"Hey, babe," Dean says, coming over and kissing me hard. "Luke has tickets for Joe. Can you give them to him tonight?"

"Sure," I reply, trying to hold my voice steady.

Dean turns back to the desk to retrieve the tickets when Kane clears his throat.

"Are you going to introduce us?" he asks Dean, smiling.

"Oh, sorry." After handing me the tickets, Dean wraps his arm around my waist. "Kane Cassidy, this is my girlfriend, Olivia Darrow."

"It's nice to meet you." Kane extends his hand for me to shake. "Dean's mentioned you a few times, but he never disclosed how beautiful you are."

I simply smile as anxiety takes hold of every cell in my body.

"Kane's company is one of our promoters," Dean explains, grinning with pride. "We're going over some last-minute items before tomorrow since Luke is still down at CSB headquarters with his lawyer."

"I heard about the young woman who worked in his club being murdered," Kane says, his gaze never leaving me. "Tragic that such a young life could be cutdown so short. The chief of CSB is a personal friend of my father's. He mentioned that they have a possible suspect, but are waiting for the evidence to be located before charging him."

"I hope it's not Luke." Dean chuckles. "I don't want to be out of a job just after starting."

"No, that's not whose name I heard the chief mention," Kane says, his eyes boring into mine. "It's someone by the name of Michael Darrow. Is he your father, Olivia? I would assume so as you both have the same last name, but I could be wrong."

"Yes, he is, but he didn't do it," I reply, my rage building.

"That's why she was taken off the case," Dean adds, much to my astonishment. "Olivia is a homicide detective for CSB and the Marsh murder was originally hers, but because of her father's ties she was placed on leave."

I close my eyes to disguise my anger as I feel my face reddening. Dean shouldn't be discussing things like this with such ease and lack of regard to how it might be making me feel.

"That's horrible," Kane says, pretending to be shocked. "This must be a really difficult time for you."

"I'm managing," I retort, then change my focus solely to Dean. "I have to get back to the club."

Dean kisses me passionately. "Are you wearing the bikini tonight?" he asks with a devilish smile.

"Unfortunately."

"Take a picture and send it to me." He nuzzles my neck. "I want to be able to relish how you look in it since I can't be there."

I force a grin, then step into the hallway, closing the door behind me. I mutter to myself as I make my way back to Verdigris, both upset and angry by what just happened. Kane mentioned my father and the case on purpose, I just wish I knew why. There's no reason for him to have done that unless he was trying to provoke some sort of response from Dean.

That asshole better keep his mouth shut about what happened between us at Requiem, otherwise his death will be the next one that gets investigated.

I storm into Joe's office, which is empty, slap the tickets on his desk, then as I turn to leave something written on them catches my attention. There are two promoters listed, one of them being BluTrend Technologies, which doesn't surprise me since that's the company Kane works for and his father owns. What does cause me to pause is the name listed for the second promoter: Centurion. It's the same company that owns Requiem. I wouldn't expect them to be able to afford to foot the bill for the fight knowing the types of properties they have. Frank did say they're part of a conglomeration, so the company could be owned by any dozens of other wealthier ones.

Deciding not to worry about it for the moment, I head up to the apartment to get ready, which I prolong for as long as possible. I take a shower even though I took one this morning, then don the horrid bikini, including my typical pasties and groan in disgust when I glance at my reflection in the mirror in the bathroom. I put my hair in a braid, and decide against my better judgement and take the picture Dean wanted, sending it to him. When I reach the bottom of the stairs Nikki is waiting for me in her typical red outfit with a white garter in her hand.

"Here." She hands it to me. "This will help you hold tips."

"Thanks," I mumble, then slip it on my leg. "This is so humiliating."

"It won't be as bad as you think," she says, smiling. "I've got something to make it easier for you if you want."

"I can't. It's against CSB regulation."

"Well, let me know if you change your mind."

She heads off to the pods when we hit the floor while I claim a tray from a cart by the bar and begin making my way around the floor, taking orders from the few people who've started trickling in. It doesn't take long for the club to fill as well as for me to be slapped on the ass a handful of times, pinched, whistled at, groped, and have money placed directly into my thong.

"Having fun?" Alice asks, filling my drink orders.

"I'm going to fucking kill Dean if I make it through tonight."

"It's not any better back here." She nods toward the rowdy men ogling her. "The bouncers have already had their hands full and it's not even eleven yet."

"I hate this shit."

"You and me both," she says, setting the drinks on my tray.

I deliver them before taking a brief rest on a stool next to Henry, which he's keeping guarded just for us ladies to use.

"You all right, hun?" he asks as I rest my head on his shoulder.

"I just want this nightmare to be over."

"I know. I'll have a discussion with Joe about his treatment of you. This is that young man's fault, so you shouldn't be punished for his temper. You do a lot for Joe and he better realize that before it's too late."

"Thanks, Henry."

I lift my head to glance around the room and scowl as Kane saunters down the steps. "I have to get back to work," I mumble, picking up my tray and heading as far from the bar as possible before I'm spotted.

I go around the floor, retaking drink orders and when I'm back at the bar Kane isn't anywhere in sight. Chloe, the other bartender, is placing my drinks on the tray when Joe comes over to me, smiling. A pit forms in my stomach.

"You're free, Olivia," he says. "You can go back up to the apartment and change into your bartender's uniform. Dean's debt has been paid in full."

I glance around the room noticing Kane lurking by the door to the back, a smug expression on his face. "Did *he* pay you?" I ask, nodding in Kane's direction.

"As a matter of fact he did, but I still need you to work. I've already pulled one of the girls from the front to cover your tables. Get going as these two need your help."

I simmer as I relinquish my tray, then make my way to the door Kane is still standing beside. Ignoring him leering at me, I pass him and head up the stairs with him quick on my heals.

"Don't I get a thank you?" he asks behind me.

"Thank you. Now go away," I reply.

"I'd thought you'd be happy you no longer have to put up with that trash touching you as I know it made you uncomfortable. I could see it on your face."

"What do you want, Kane? A gold medal?"

"What's with the attitude?" he asks, grabbing my arm as I reach the landing for the top floor.

"I could say the same thing to you about yesterday," I counter, pulling out of his grasp.

"That was business, Liv. I had to keep it professional in front of Joe."

"That's bullshit and you know it," I say, barreling through the door for the apartment. "Paying Joe to keep me off the floor isn't professional, it's demeaning. Like how you made me feel yesterday with your coldness. You fuck me one day, then treat me like garbage the next. If all you wanted was to get between my legs, well you succeeded and now you can leave."

"I'm sorry you felt that way, but that was never my intention," he says, frustrated, leaning on the doorframe for the front door, which lies open. "I thought you'd be delighted with my gesture. After you left the arena, Dean told me what happened the other night, so I thought I'd do you a favor and pay off his debt to get you out of the predicament he placed you in. But if you want those men to continue pawing you, then by all means go back downstairs in that outfit."

"What do you want, Kane? Besides humiliating me."

"I'd never do that," he says, irritated.

"Really? Then what the fuck was that crap back at Ataxia earlier? Did you enjoy dragging me through the mud for your sheer amusement? Because it sure looked like you did. Were you hoping Dean would be shocked by the information about my father?"

"I didn't even know it was *you* he was referring to as his girlfriend during our discussions. He never mentioned your name. How was I supposed to know you two are dating?" he says, slamming the door closed after stepping inside.

"We're not."

"Well he thinks you are."

"Then that's his problem," I grouse, grabbing the mini dress with its matching thong off a pile of clothes on the floor at the foot of the bed, then step into the bathroom to change, making sure the door is closed and locked.

I pull off the garter, sending the crinkled bills scattering across the floor, but I'm too enraged to bother with them for the moment. I'm so frazzled I'm having difficulty removing the bikini. I sit on the edge of the bathtub to try to calm down.

"Olivia," Kane says after knocking on the door, "I'm sorry. I don't know what I was thinking. Please come out here so we can talk about this."

"I have nothing to say to you."

"Fine."

I hear the front door open and slam shut.

I take some deep breaths before changing. I leave the heels on and my hair braided, then quickly make my way back to the club floor before Joe sends out a search party. Alice and Chloe are busy with orders from the waitresses, so I'm tasked with taking care of those sitting at the bar. Kane emerges from the back, then sits on a freshly vacated bar stool, but I ignore him and ask one of the other girls to tend to him. There's a brief lull, and I take this moment to clean some of the glasses that have begun piling up since we're running low. Unfortunately that puts me right in front of Kane, who's sipping on his drink.

"I spoke with Joe," he says, trying to get my attention. "He's giving you tomorrow night off."

"What the hell for?" I grouse.

"So you can go to the fight with me."

"I'm not going anywhere with you."

"Olivia, come on. Stop pretending to be mad."

"Who says I'm pretending?"

"What can I do to make it up to you?" he asks, turning on the charm.

"Nothing, Kane. I don't want or need anything from you. I did my job, we had some fun, now it's time for the both of us to move on."

"What if I don't want to move on from you?" he asks, wrapping his hand around my wrist.

"I can't, Kane. I don't do relationships."

"Maybe not with Dean, but that's because he doesn't deserve you. I can give you everything he can't and more. You wouldn't have to keep working in this shithole just to scrape by. Go on a few dates with me, and if it doesn't work out, then we'll go our separate ways."

"And the first place you want to take me is where Dean works?" I ask. "He'd kill us both if he saw me with you."

"Not when I have a private box above the stands. There will be dozens of people with us, and he'll be too busy taking care of security on the floor he won't even know you're in the building."

I know this is a bad idea, but when have I ever made a rational decision? "I'll need to think about it."

He smiles, releasing me so I can continue washing the glasses. A fresh wave of patrons stumble in, throwing Alice, Chloe, and me back into a frenzy. I don't notice Kane is gone until I clear the glass from his seat. By the time the last person leaves it's nearly three in the morning and I'm dead tired. I tell Alice and Chloe to divide the tips between the two of them before I make my way up to the apartment. When I open the door rose petals are strewn all over the floor as candles burn on the tables and countertops for the kitchen. It takes a few seconds for my eyes to adjust, and I spot Kane standing off to the side holding a bouquet of roses.

"I thought, perhaps, this would be a better first date than the fight," he says, stepping behind me, closing the door.

"How did you get up here after you left?"

"Joe gave me the access code for the alley door. It's clear he wants us to try this relationship out."

"That's because he hates Dean."

"How lucky for me." Taking my hand, Kane sets the roses on the couch.

He brings me over to the bed, has me lie down, then proceeds to remove my heels while his mouth slowly makes its way up my leg and his hands tug off the thong. When his tongue finds its way inside of me, I moan, then discard the mini dress and remove the pasties, dropping them onto the floor. Kane kisses me as I work on getting his clothes off. He suckles my breasts before penetrating me and I cry out in pleasure. After bending my knees, I lift my legs so he can get deeper inside and moan louder with each passing second hoping our time together doesn't end. Kane cries out my name as he comes, sweat soaking our bodies. As he moves us toward the head of the bed, we start over. We grow exhausted as the minutes past from the hectic night, but neither of us is refusing to slow or even stop. It's not long until I finally climax, then he plasters himself against my back, pulling the sheets over our tired bodies, and we promptly fall asleep.

Eight

I'm roused by Kane stroking my back, his mouth nuzzling my neck. He fucks me incessantly the moment he notices I'm awake, and I enjoy every minute of it.

"I just can't get enough of you, Olivia," he whispers as my body tightens, his orgasm causing mine.

He kisses me hard as my cell phone begins to ring. I ignore it, but the noise seems to intrigue Kane, who reaches for the device, which sits on the nightstand beside the bed.

"Don't," I say, trying to grab it from him.

"Are you afraid it might be Dean?" he asks, teasing, holding the phone out of reach as he lies on top of me. He bends his wrist so he can read the screen. "It *is* the boyfriend and it's a video call. Shall we answer it?"

"No," I reply, panicking. "Please, Kane, don't."

"I'm not going to, sweetheart," he says, dropping the phone onto the floor. "I wouldn't put you through that kind of embarrassment or harm. Why don't we get dressed and I'll take you to my estate for the day? We can lounge around the pool in the nice warm sun until it's time to leave for the fight."

"What time does it begin?"

"Eight, but I'll need to be there beforehand to greet the fighters. I'll have you wait in my private box that way Dean won't know you're in the building."

"I'll need to stop by my house to pick up something to wear."

"Brooke has plenty of clothes you can borrow."

He gets up and heads into the bathroom to take a brief shower while I stay in bed. My phone beeps, alerting me that a message was left, so I retrieve it, unlock the screen, and play Dean's message.

"Hey, babe," he begins, smiling wide. "Your picture served me well last night. I can't wait to see you in that outfit in person. I'm going to be unavailable all day today. This is my one chance to call and tell you how much I love you and how I look forward to seeing you at home tomorrow."

Dread fills my soul as I shutoff the phone, placing it on the nightstand. Sitting up, I pull my knees to my chest as I drape the sheet over my chilled body. I'm screwing everything up by being with Kane, but I never really asked to be in a relationship with Dean in the first place. He put me in this predicament by pushing his way into my life after years of me saying no. If only he listened, the pain that's going to befall both of us could've been prevented. This is going to come to a crashing end soon, I can feel it. I just hope I can survive the damage that's going to be caused.

"Hey, you okay?" Kane asks, sitting on the side of the bed.

"I'm fine," I respond. "Let me get cleaned up and we'll go."

He kisses me before I get out of bed to head into the bathroom where I take a nice, hot shower. When I step out, Kane is dressed and standing over by the boxes looking at the photos taped to the wall.

"What's this?" he asks as I dress.

"A few cases I'm helping one of the SVU detectives with," I reply, joining him. "I hate being idle and my supervisor gave me permission to look these over."

"I would've thought there'd be more people missing in Asmor."

"There are, it's just the detective in charge feels these five are related, but I haven't been able to determine how yet." I go around the apartment blowing out any of the candles that are still burning from last night.

Grabbing my purse, which I'd shoved into one of my bags, I place my credentials, wallet, cell phone, and gun inside.

"Do you always carry that with you?" Kane asks, referring to the weapon.

"I have to. It's part of CSB regulations that an officer must always have their service weapon on hand even when not on duty."

"Good to know."

We make our way down to the main floor, then out into the alley. Kane's car, which is a two-door, dark blue sports car, is sitting only a few feet away. He opens the passenger side door for me before sliding behind the wheel, moving us out of Nok. We speed through Hunnat, then into Crer, and eventually out into the open landscape that surrounds a few of the sectors. After leaving Crer, it takes us about twenty minutes to reach the checkpoint for the bridge that goes into Waterside. The guard's computers recognize Kane's license plate, which automatically lifts up the gate for us to pass. If I was in my vehicle, I'd have to flash my credentials to gain access. Those who work on the island have special markers on their cars identifying them, and guests have to be added to a list at the gate. Everyone else is barred from simply wandering onto the island.

The bridge spans seven miles across azure-colored waters. It's four lanes and barely has any traffic on it for a Saturday morning. The sun shines brilliantly overhead, so Kane rolls down the windows to let the salty sea air waft in. I become more relaxed the farther we get away from the mainland. Kane takes hold of my hand, squeezing it as we come to the halfway point passing a lighthouse on our left. When we reach the end we come upon a stoplight and have to wait to make a left turn onto Trent, which is the first street on the island. We next hang a right onto Sycamore, taking that clear across to the western edge where we turn left onto Highland, another left onto Montgomery, then finally a right onto Wells. The Cassidy estate marks the end of the street, its terracotta roof expanding outward from a carport we pull onto. Kane whips the car around, parking it in a three-car garage on the left while another sits on the right of the carport with a magnificent and sprawling rose garden filling in the space between the garage and the house.

Grasping my hand, he guides me up the entryway and into a grand foyer that stretches two stories high, though from the looks of the interior the house is only one level. The smell of freshly cooked food makes its way over to us, causing me to almost drool.

"They're probably eating in the kitchen." Kane nods his head toward a bend to the left off a sunken living room just beyond the foyer.

We step up into an immaculate kitchen with a wet bar on the right and a dinette nestled in the corner while the cabinets, countertops, and appliances are all housed to the left. The table has been nicely prepared with dishes of eggs, bacon, toast, fruit, and a carafe filled with juice. Richard Cassidy sits rather rigid in his seat, his suit crinkling as his face does when he spots us, then forces himself to smile. Brooke sits beside him with a dour expression concealing something that borders on resentment.

"I wasn't expecting company," Richard says as nicely as his acidic tone will allow, which is completely opposite of our first encounter.

"Olivia and I will be spending the day here until the fight tonight," Kane says, ignoring his father's attitude. He pulls the chair closest to Brooke out for me, then takes the one by his father as a housekeeper sets plates down in front of us.

"What time do you plan on leaving?" Brooke asks, her bloodshot eyes boring into me. She's too thin to be healthy, now that I see her up close. Her blond hair hangs loose around her shoulders while the top she has on cuts deep down her chest, making it obvious that she's not wearing a bra.

"Not for hours, Brooke," Kane replies, annoyed. "If you're that bothered by Olivia being here, go hide in your room like you always do. She did you a favor and saved your life, if you actually gave a damn about it."

"No one asked her to interfere." Brooke slams her fork down, nearly chipping the porcelain of her dish, but she keeps the utensil clutched in her finely manicured fingers.

"I did," Richard retorts, his face hard as stone. "No child of mine will ever disgrace this family, and I'll do everything in my power and means to ensure that such an event never takes place. Even if it does mean calling in CSB." His last comment is clearly aimed at Frank's interference.

"If Olivia's supervisor didn't track her, who knows what that crazy asshole would've done," Kane says, coming to my defense. "We've had this discussion enough already, Richard. It's over and done with. Move on before you say something you'll regret."

Tensions are high, making me very uncomfortable, but I have no means of escape. I'm a little awestruck how Kane referred to his father by his first name, but it's not unheard of among the wealthier community that parents are often regarded as equals, not overseers. I've called my father by his first name before, but that's only when I've been angry or upset, never in casual discussion.

Brooke continues to stare at me, but the hostility she was emitting begins to wane. "What do you do for CSB?" she asks after a few minutes.

"I'm a homicide detective," I reply, eating my food slowly as I feel uncomfortable.

"Do you like that kind of work?"

"I enjoy the mystery of it. A puzzle needing to be solved. It intrigues me what goes through the human mind when they're taking someone's life."

Richard glares at me. "I'm sure your appetite for it came about because of the death of your mother."

"Yes, it did," I reply, glowering.

"How old were you when she died?" Brooke asks.

"I was six."

"That's the same age I was when my mother died."

"Yes, but yours overdosed, whereas, Olivia's mother was murdered."

"Did they ever catch the person?"

"No, they didn't."

"Pity," Richard says, snickering, which bothers me tremendously. "Are you still planning on having your post-fight celebration here tomorrow night, Kane?"

"Yes. Mabel is working with the caterers and the rest of the staff."

The housekeeper wanders over to the table at the mention of her name. She's a plump, older woman with graying hair swept up into a bun.

"Everything has been arranged, Mr. Cassidy," she says, addressing Kane. "The decorators will be here at noon, and the caterers an hour later. I've got everything handled."

"As always, Mabel, you're perfect," Kane says, smiling. "Olivia, why don't you stay the night? That way you'll already be here for when the festivities begin and you won't have to commute back and forth from Range."

"I don't have anything with me."

"You can borrow my clothes," Brooke chimes in, perking up. "I've got plenty of things for you to wear."

"Then it's settled," Richard says, finally beginning to relax.

I'm not sure what to make of everyone's change in attitude toward me, but at least the tension is gone.

Richard excuses himself a few minutes later and is soon followed by Brooke. When Kane and I are done eating, I follow him back toward the foyer, but we turn down a hallway on our right before we get near it. The first door we come to on our left opens into an expansive bedroom with a vaulted ceiling, a walk-in closet, and a bathroom almost the size of my entire house with a sunken tub and glass shower stall. The lone window in the bedroom on the far wall overlooks the carport.

"This is my room," Kane says. "My father kept the master suite after Brooke's mother died. Brooke's room is just down the hall, and there's a guest room next to hers. Of course, you'll be staying in here with me." He wraps his arms around my waist, kissing me gently on the lips. "Let's head out to the pool. I'll get you something to wear from my closet." He steps away and emerges with two soft, black robes, handing one to me.

I eye him with suspicion. "Won't I need a swimsuit?"

"No," he replies, winking.

"And if your father or sister should happen to come outside, what then?"

"Then I guess they'll get more than they bargained for," he replies, laughing. "It'll be fine, Olivia. Richard won't bother us and

Brooke won't care if she sees anything. Loosen up, Detective. Things are a lot more relaxed here on Waterside than the mainland."

He tosses the robes onto the bed and begins to remove my clothes, his mouth caressing my body as he goes. When he's done, I slip on the robe while he undresses, and the two of us make our way back toward the kitchen and into a family room that has an entrance onto a covered lanai, which extends outwards to the pool at the far end of the property. Kane drops his robe onto the stone surrounding the pool before jumping in. I'm a little hesitant, but with some coaxing I follow suit. We splash around for a few minutes before he pulls me into his arms. He pins me against the side of the pool, his hands cupping my breasts as he takes me from behind.

"Stay with me, Olivia," Kane whispers. "You belong here."

"I can't," I moan.

"Is it because of Dean?"

"Yes," I admit seconds before I climax.

"We'll have to remedy that." Kane turns me to face him, his mouth covering mine.

He moves me over to the sun shelf along the front of the pool, gently guiding me up the thin steps, then lying me flat on my back so he can have me again. I know I'm being put on display, but I'm too caught up in Kane to care. I feel at ease in his arms and wanted like never before. Kane could do anything to me in this moment and I'd relish the attention. I don't want to be anywhere else, not just now, perhaps ever.

When we finish, Kane brings me over to a cabana by the lanai where we lie down under its shade. My head rests on his chest, and I feel myself drifting off. Kane rouses me when lunch is ready. He tosses me the robe after donning his own and we head inside. Like this morning, Richard and Brooke are sitting at the dinette when we join them. We're in the middle of a delightful conversation when Mabel interrupts.

"Excuse me, Mr. Cassidy, but Luke Cobb is at the door requesting to speak with you."

"Escort him into the living room and tell him I'll be along shortly." As Mabel turns, Kane touches her arm for her to stop. "Is he alone?"

"No, sir. There's another gentleman with him."

"Have them both wait for me in the living room," Kane says as my nerves begin to shake.

"Shit," I mutter after she's left.

"You don't know it's Dean," Kane says.

"Who's Dean?" Brooke asks.

"Someone I'd like to avoid," I reply.

"Brooke, why don't you take Olivia into your room while your brother meets with these men?" Richard suggests.

"That's not a bad idea," Kane says in agreement. "They can't see you from the living room when you're heading down the hallway to our bedrooms. You should be fine there."

Brooke and I take our plates before making our way toward her room, which is along a hallway opposite from her brother's. She closes the door as I sit on a loveseat with her sitting beside me.

"I take it Dean is an old boyfriend," Brooke says as I continue to tremble.

"And one with a horrible temper."

"I've had plenty of those."

"Was Riddle one of them?"

"Unfortunately," she says, rolling her eyes.

"Why were you at Requiem for so long?"

"To escape this place."

"It can't be that terrible to live here."

"Probably if you're not a Cassidy, but my father has high expectations for his children and I don't exactly fall under that umbrella like Kane does. They both have a tendency to be overly critical about my choices in life, which pushes me over the edge sometimes."

127

"At least your father cares about you. Mine shut down after my mother died, leaving me to my own devices, which weren't always legal ones."

This causes Brooke to laugh.

I set my empty plate onto a small table, then stand and wander around her room, looking at the dozens of photos she has in a collage above her dresser. One picture catches my attention and I feel sickened by a possible revelation.

"Who's in this photo?" I ask, pointing to one along the bottom, trying to hide my unease.

"Oh, that's me and one of my club friends, Erin." Brooke sets her plate down before joining me. "I met her at Temptation a little over five years ago." Her face darkens. "She's been missing for the last few years though."

I study the picture very carefully before I utter my next comment. "You two could be mistaken for sisters."

"We got that all the time," Brooke says, removing the picture, holding it in her hand. "Sometimes we used it to our advantage. Mainly when it came to getting guys to buy us drinks. She was of age, but I wasn't. Of course, it didn't stop anyone at the club from plying us with alcohol, especially when additional favors were promised or involved. I just thought she got tired of the club scene until I heard rumors going around after Temptation closed that she'd disappeared."

"Would you excuse me for a minute, Brooke?"

"Sure."

Slipping out of her room, I make my way back to Kane's where I retrieve my cell phone to make a call.

"Rodgers," Gail answers after the first ring.

"It's Olivia. Have you been able to discover anything from the Hub about a possible glitch when your women were taken?"

"According to them, everything was working perfectly. It's like I suspected. Their microchips simply stopped functioning. Why? You sound like you've got something."

"Do you have DNA on any of the victims? Maybe something from a toothbrush or comb."

"Yeah, why?" I can hear her sitting up straighter.

"Run them against each other and see if you find a familial match."

"What would I compare the results to if they come back as related?"

"Pull Brooke Cassidy's records from Grove Hospital. She was there a few days ago, so they'll have her profile in their system."

"Cassidy? As in Richard Cassidy's daughter? Are you sure?" Gail asks, her voice tensing up.

"Yes, Gail, I'm sure. Brooke has a picture of herself with Erin Carr, the second missing persons case you gave me. The two women are practically identical. It's scary. It may not help find these women, but now you'll have your suspicions confirmed about why you feel they're connected. It could open a door you never knew existed. Once you have the profile, run it against all missing persons. This may only be the tip of the iceberg if my hunch is correct."

"Olivia, what have we gotten ourselves into?"

"I don't want to think about that right now. Let me know what you discover."

I end the call just as Kane enters, grousing.

"I don't believe this shit," he grumbles, heading toward the bathroom. "You'd think money would take care of everything, but all it does is serve to rouse the greedy assholes out of their slumber."

"What happened?" I ask, leaning against the doorframe as he steps into the shower.

"A manager for one of the boxers is upping his price to permit his man to fight. He knows how much revenue is being generated and the bastard wants more than he's worth to fulfill the contract he signed. Luke and Dean are heading to Ataxia, and I'm to meet them there. I'll have to come back to pick you up for the fight."

"So, it *was* Dean who was with him."

"Yes, which is another reason I want you to stay here," he says, emerging to grab a towel off a rack by the stall. "Hopefully this won't take too long and we can have dinner before the fight. Brooke will keep you company in my absence. I'll call you when I'm on my way back."

He rushes into his closet, dresses, and leaves without saying another word. I put my phone back into my purse before returning to Brooke's room where we spend the next hour going through her closet. Of the hundreds of outfits she has, the one that fits me the best is a short, blue-sequined sleeveless dress with straps that crisscross down the exposed back. The shoes she has to go with it are a little tight, but they'll have to do. I take the garment into Kane's room, then draw myself a bath, sinking as far down into the tub as I can while the jets pulsate against my tight skin. I stay in longer than I should, and as I'm wrapping a towel around my body my cell phone begins to ring in the other room. I barely answer it in time.

"We're not going to be able to make dinner," Kane says. "This bastard won't give in, so I'm having to get our lawyers involved."

"Will the fight still go on?"

"It will. I'll make sure of that as I have too much invested to allow it to fail. My father will bring you to the arena. There will be cocktails starting at six in my private box along with some finger foods, so at least we won't go hungry. I'll make us a proper meal when we return home tonight." Kane says it so casually it almost slips past my notice. I told him I don't do relationships and here he's making it sound like we're living together. "Text me when you're here."

He hangs up before I get a chance to respond. I grumble as I look at the time on the phone's screen, noticing it's nearly five. It'll take us well over an hour to reach the arena, or longer depending upon traffic. I dry off, slip the dress and shoes on, then ask Brooke if I can borrow some makeup.

"What are you going to do tonight?" I ask as she watches me primp.

"I have a friend coming over in a little while. We'll probably just stay here and watch a movie or something."

I thank her for letting me borrow the dress and makeup, then run a comb through my hair before retrieving my purse and meeting Richard in the foyer. I'm put off by the grin on his face when I come into his view. It makes me squirm, so I hide it as best I can while we make our way to the garage where Kane parked his car. Richard drives an older model with a leather interior and wood accents, but still very sleek and stylish. It's not long until we're crossing the bridge heading toward the mainland. I'm grateful for the silence, but unsettled by it as well. Richard obviously has something on his mind as he bites his lower lip to keep quiet.

"My son is quite taken with you," he says, sounding slightly worried. "It doesn't take much for him to wrap his life around a pretty face."

Ignoring the comment, I continue to gaze out the window beside me.

"I wouldn't get too comfortable in our house, Olivia. Kane will eventually grow tired of you like he has with all his other girlfriends."

"I have no intentions on becoming comfortable in your home," I say, trying to sound snide. "The commute to CSB would be too long."

"I've met many women in your position. They're usually willing to do anything to keep their claws in a man with money and position. I'm sure a lot of that behavior is learned from their mothers. Yours included even if you were young at the time of her death."

My blood begins to boil as I feel the bulge of my weapon in my purse pressing against my hand, begging to be used.

"You know nothing about my mother," I retort, choking back tears.

"I know more about her than you could possibly imagine," he says, smiling. "For instance, did you know she worked for me right up until she was murdered? She was my secretary for several years, even before you were born. She loathed her home life until you came along, but even after that she tried everything to improve her situation. Perhaps it's what got her killed."

131

"What are you hoping to accomplish by telling me these things? Other than to piss me off."

"I'm just putting you on your guard. It's my way of letting you know I don't approve of your relationship with Kane, and since he won't listen to me I'm hoping you will."

"I'm not in a relationship with your son, so you have nothing to worry about."

"We'll see about that. Kane is the type of man that when he finds something he wants there's no stopping him in obtaining it. And what my son wants more than anything in life right now is you."

I don't know how to reply, or even if I should, so I simply sit in silence and allow my anger to simmer. With being at Ataxia I'll be close to the club to return to before the night is over. I refuse to be fodder for this man's amusement, regardless of the feelings his son may have for me or those I have begun to develop for him. I don't need this kind of toxic shit in my life. My father and Dean give me enough of that already.

When we reach Nok the line of cars heading toward the arena is very evident, but like everything else in our society they're segregated with those arriving from Waterside given the advantage at first priority. Richard pulls the car up to the valet, hands over his keys to the young man, then wraps my arm in his as he escorts me through the front doors, flash bulbs going off in our faces from reporters camped only feet away. We pass through and are immediately met by security officers and metal detectors. My purse is searched, and when they notice the gun I make it a point to display my CSB credentials. I pass through the inspection with ease after going through the detector to make sure I'm not carrying anything else under this short, tight dress and am permitted to keep my weapon.

We turn left, heading toward the bank of elevators that'll take us up to the box level. BluTrend Technologies has box two hundred reserved, which is the first set of doors we come to on our right after stepping off the elevator. There's already a handful of people inside, all of them strangers to me. Richard leaves me standing by the doorway while he makes his introductions around the room. I move off to the side to be out of the way as I feel out of place without

Kane here. The situation only intensifies when my cell phone begins ringing. Dean's name scrolling across the screen.

"Hello?" I ask in a hushed tone.

"Why the hell are you here?" he replies, furious.

"How'd you know?"

"Because I was alerted when you flashed your credentials at the door. I thought you were working at the club tonight?"

"Joe gave me the night off so I can attend the fight with one of his clients."

"I know you walked in with Richard Cassidy, so don't lie to me about who you're here with. Did Kane invite you?"

"No, Dean."

"Are you sure? I saw the way he was looking at you when I introduced the two of you the other day."

"I came with Richard because he's a client of Joe's. He hired me for the missing persons case I was working a few days ago. The one I told you about."

"You made me look like a fool, Liv. Pretending you didn't know who Kane Cassidy was."

"I didn't until that day. I'd strictly been dealing with his father. Dean, you're making something out of nothing. Richard is just thanking me for doing my job successfully."

"Are you fucking him?"

"What?" I utter, stunned by the question. "Why would you ask such a thing?"

"Just answer the damn question!" he screams.

"No, asshole, I'm not. What the hell is wrong with you?"

"Make sure you leave Ataxia alone. I don't want to see you with either of the Cassidy men after tonight, is that understood?"

"Who the hell do you think you are? You can't tell me what to do."

"Don't piss me off any further, Liv. You won't like it."

The call ends, and I want nothing more than to run from this place. Quickly looking around, I notice Richard is over by the windows overlooking the arena floor, his attention being paid to a lovely, young woman who can't be too much older than Brooke. I take this as my opportunity to slip from the room, but as I approach the elevators Kane emerges, smiling when he sees me.

"Dean knows I'm here." I try to step past him and onto the elevator, but Kane grabs my arm to stop me.

"How do you know?"

"He called me. I told him I came here with your father, but he's still furious. I have to leave."

"No, Olivia, you don't. I can take care of this."

"Dean isn't the only reason I'm going," I say, pulling out of his grasp.

"What do you mean?" he asks, looking genuinely hurt.

"Ask your father."

"God damn it," Kane utters. "I'm going to kill that asshole. He can never leave my life alone. Especially when it has to do with someone I care very much about."

"You barely know me, Kane. I hardly know you. It's just best if we end this now."

"Please, Olivia," he takes my hands in his, "let me make this right. It'll all be better by tomorrow, I promise."

"Dean is more than likely watching us right now, so this is only making things worse," I say, releasing him.

"He has an entire arena to monitor. I doubt he's only focused on you."

"Then you don't know Dean."

Kane moves closer to me, so he can whisper in my ear. "Stay, Olivia." His hot breath tickles my ear as heat builds between us. "I can protect you like no one else, and not just from men like Dean. I need you. Please don't go."

I think back to all the problems Dean has caused in my life, with the latest being the incident at Verdigris where I was degraded to the point of being forced to fuck Glen Growsky. I've always gone after men who hurt me, so maybe it's time I changed my thinking and went with what was right for once.

"All right. I'll stay."

Kane's face lights up, and as he goes to kiss me he thinks better of it, so instead we make our way back to the box where more people have joined the party. Kane keeps me close to his side as a waitress goes around passing out cocktails and hors d'oeuvres. He introduces me to those who are on the board for BluTrend, their wives or husbands, and everyone else in the room. He places his hand on the small of my back, clearly not afraid of what the security camera in the corner of the room is transmitting to those spying on us on the floor below. The more I drink, the more relaxed I become and less worried about Dean. Kane assures me every so often that Luke has Dean too busy that he won't have time to barge into the box and bother our good time. Also it would cost Dean his job if he left his post to handle a personal matter.

The night begins to go by in a blur until it's time for the fight to begin. The lights in the box and around the arena floor dim ever so slightly as the two boxers saunter down the aisles while the announcer introduces them. Because of the thickness of the glass we can't hear the screams and shouts of those in the seats below us, only what's being broadcasted through the speakers and on the television screens scattered around the large room. Drinks are refilled as bells sound signaling the beginning of round one.

I sit close to the window, observing what I can as the fighters take to the ring while Kane is busy socializing with those more interested in drinking than watching two men beat each other's brains out. After three rounds they're both evenly matched, each with cuts along their brow lines that are being tended to by their trainers off in the corners.

"Having fun?" Kane asks, sitting beside me.

"It's all right. Did you bet on either of them?"

"No, as I get paid regardless of who wins."

135

"What kind of profit will this net BluTrend and Centurion?"

He raises an eyebrow when I mention the name of the other sponsor. "You're very observant."

"I saw it listed on the tickets Joe was given."

"BluTrend will receive the most since we put in the most while Centurion will simply be recouping the money they invested with only the slightest increase in revenue."

"I take it they're not a large company."

"Their participation in all of this was mainly a way to generate exposure to the clubs they own, nothing more."

"Do you know who runs the company?"

"Luke and I have only dealt with their lawyer while we were working on bringing the fight into Asmor, so I'm not sure who actually sits behind the big chair over there."

The bell rings again, signaling the beginning of round four. Kane's hand slips under the straps for the dress along my back, his fingers sliding down my spine. He takes his other hand to brush my hair away, then begins to nuzzle my neck. In an instant my cell phone rings and I know immediately who it is. Reaching into my purse, Kane snatches the phone before I can, then promptly answers it.

"Dean, Olivia is busy at the moment," Kane says as he stands and steps away, but not too far. "I know you're watching, but do I need to remind you of the job Luke hired you to perform. There are over forty-thousand people in this arena and they're all depending on you to keep them safe. Stop focusing on one individual and do your fucking job." He pauses, and I can hear Dean ranting on the other end, but I can't understand what he's saying. "Consider this your breakup notice." Kane hangs up the phone, then scrolls through my contacts. It isn't until he returns the phone to me do I realize he's blocked Dean's number. "That should take care of things."

"Or make them worse," I grouse.

"You need to trust me, Olivia." Kane looks deep into my eyes. "I'm all you'll ever need." He kisses me hard, and it takes all of our willpower not to fuck each other in front of everyone.

136

Again, my phone starts to ring, but it's from a number I don't recognize. Kane is obviously annoyed by the interruption, so he uses his cell to call Luke, threatening to pull any future sponsorship from all events if Dean doesn't leave me alone. My phone goes silent. I should feel relieved, but fear grips me instead because Dean isn't the type of person to leave any betrayal alone. And that's exactly how he'll perceive tonight. Kane may think he's doing me a favor, but in reality he's placed my life in grave danger.

"Why don't we head back to Waterside?" Kane suggests when he notices my distress.

"All right," I say rather quickly, desperate to put this place behind me.

Kane calls down to the valet station and orders his car so it'll be waiting for us when we arrive downstairs. He informs Richard that we're leaving, says good-bye to a few people, then hurries me out the door. I know Dean is tracking our movements, so I'm not surprised when the elevator doors open on the first level and I spot him trying to barrel his way through throngs of people watching the fight on the screens along the outer hallway. Kane and I make our way outside and into his car before Dean can reach us. I tremble during the entire drive and can't seem to stop even when we're back at the estate.

"Why don't you get out of the dress and put on the robe from earlier while I get dinner going?" Kane says after we enter the house.

I nod, then turn down the hallway that'll take me to his room. The minute the door is closed, I sit on the edge of the bed to take off the shoes since they're killing my feet, but I also remove my cell phone from my purse. Kane didn't notice when I placed the ringer on silent after Dean's last call attempt, and as I look over the screen a voice message from a number I don't recognize flashes across. I know I shouldn't listen to it, but this isn't how I wanted to end things with Dean. If I'm honest with myself, I didn't want to stop seeing him. The decision was made without my consent, so I feel I owe him enough to at least hear what he has to say no matter how painful it's going to be.

"Liv, what the hell just happened?" he begins, his tone one of confusion instead of fury. "We're over just like that? Was that your idea or Kane's? I don't want to believe it was yours because this isn't like you. I've known you too long, Olivia. This is out of character. I need you to talk to me, not that fucking asshole. I love you, please tell me what's going on. Your phone isn't accepting my calls anymore, so I can only assume that bastard blocked me, but you can easily remedy that. I need to see you, Liv. Call me when you're alone. We can fix whatever you think is broken. I love you, please don't cut me out."

Tears stream down my cheeks as I wasn't expecting Dean's message to be calm and coherent. He should've been raving, screaming and yelling about what a horrible person I am, but he sounded broken and scared. That is greatly out of character for him. He's right that he's known me so long to understand what transpired tonight wasn't by my hand. I scroll through my contacts to find Dean's name, but I hesitate in unblocking his number. Something tells me Kane will check my phone and that he'll want to listen to the message Dean left if he notices it.

Deleting the message out of fear, I put the ringer back on, tuck my phone deep into the purse, and discard the dress, putting on the soft black robe. I step into the bathroom to wash my face, mainly to hide the fact that I've been crying as it'll cause Kane to ask why. As soon as I'm presentable, I join him in the kitchen. We eat a light dinner of salmon and rice, then retreat to bed where we make love well into the night.

Nine

"How was the fight?" Brooke asks as we sit down to breakfast.

"Your brother didn't stay for too much of it," Richard comments, with clear disdain. "But the top ranked boxer won after landing a knockout punch in the sixth round."

"My part was already done by the time the fight started, so I really didn't need to be there any longer," Kane counters. "Where were you, by the way, Brooke? You weren't home when we returned."

"I was in Nok at one of the clubs I normally frequent with a couple of my friends."

Kane scowls at her.

"It's not like I'm under house arrest," she retorts. "I am an adult, Kane, no matter how much you hate that fact."

"I don't hate that you're an adult. I just can't stand that you're an irresponsible one. Maybe having Olivia around will help change your ways."

"She's going to be living here now?" Brooke asks, shocked. I catch a hint of either anger or jealousy also in her tone, which I'm not sure what to make of.

"No, she isn't," Richard answers before I can. "At least not under this roof."

"Staying here brings me too far from CSB headquarters. Besides, I like my home in Range."

"I'm sure you do, but you were meant to live here on Waterside, Olivia," Kane says.

"No, she wasn't," Richard retorts rather forcefully. "If she was, she would've been born here."

"Olivia will be living here, Richard. I'll be damned if she's going to continue working at Verdigris just to make ends meet."

"You work at one of the clubs?" Brooke asks, her mouth falling open.

"Yes, but I also get hired for private cases. That brings in more money than anything I make at the club."

"Then why do you work there?" Kane asks.

"Because Joe has the connections I need."

"Well, you've got me now, so that can stop."

"What if I don't want it to stop, Kane?" I ask, irritated. "You're suddenly making all these decisions for me without asking. We're not a couple, and even if we were I wouldn't let you dictate my life."

I storm out of the room, heading toward the bedroom with Kane quick on my heels.

"Look, I'm sorry, Olivia." He closes the door to his bedroom after we've entered. "I'm so used to making all decisions that no one has ever questioned me about them. Sometimes it's hard to separate what I do at work to what needs to be done with my personal life. I didn't mean to upset you. I guess I'm just excited to start a life with you now that Dean is officially out of the picture."

"Stop trying to force a relationship on me," I say, my temper rising. "This isn't who I am. I'm not one of your high society rich girls who doesn't have a thought in her head except the one her boyfriend tells her to have. I speak my mind, do what the fuck I want, and have no one I need to be accountable to or for. I'm my own person, make my own rules, and live my life on my terms. I'm not what you're looking for, and you can't change me to conform into that mold you seem desperate to fill."

"I'm not desperate." His face reddens. "I love you, Olivia. All right? There, I said it. I've fallen in love with you and want you all to myself. I can't help it if that upsets you, but you've probably never had a stable relationship in your life and don't know what to do when one is presented to you."

"Don't say those things to me."

"What? That I love you? Why?"

"Because it makes me uncomfortable."

"How could knowing someone loves you make you feel uncomfortable?"

"I don't want to talk about this." I move away from him and over towards the pile of clothes I have on the floor. "You haven't even known me a week, so what you're feeling is desperation, not love. I should know. I've experienced enough of that in my life to tell the difference."

"I don't use those words loosely." Coming over to me, he tries to pull me close. "I mean every one of them, Olivia."

"You don't want me, Kane. I'm too damaged," I say, giving up the fight.

"You're perfect. My father's an asshole, and he's more than likely jealous that I have you and he doesn't. Just give this a few days and I promise you won't regret it."

I go to open my mouth to reply when my phone starts to ring, Joe's name scrolling across the screen when I retrieve it.

"Hello, Joe," I say upon answering.

"I don't know whether you pissed him off or if he's finally coming to his senses," Joe replies.

"What are you talking about?"

"Security alerted me this morning that Dean dropped off over four dozen roses to the front door of the club. All of them addressed to you."

"Really?" I ask, surprised by the gesture, as well as thrilled by it, which shocks me.

"I had them moved into the apartment you're staying in, but wasn't I surprised to find you aren't there. Shacking up with someone else?" he asks, chuckling.

"None of your business."

"Right. Tell Kane I'll see him tonight." Joe ends the call.

"Who was that?"

"Joe. Apparently your threat to Dean didn't take. He sent me dozens of roses this morning," I reply, trying desperately to hide my smile.

"And this makes you happy?" he asks, annoyed.

"Shocked, is more like it."

"You love him, don't you?"

"No, of course not."

"Yet you can't stop smiling," Kane says, his ire rising.

"He's just never done anything like this before. I'm stunned, that's all."

Kane studies me very carefully, his eyes narrowing as his arms cross his chest. "I guess the competition is going to get fierce now. I'm up for the challenge." He pulls me against him, a devilish smile appearing on his face. "Maybe we should send him a video of how I make you come over and over again. Then, perhaps, he'll get the hint."

Kane opens my robe as his mouth covers mine. It's not long until we're tangled in the sheets, our bodies covered in sweat while I beg for him not to stop.

The caterers arrive just before one, and the entire house is placed into immediate chaos. Kane, Richard, and Mabel are busy getting the house ready for the party that's scheduled to start at seven, while I take a relaxing soak in the tub and Brooke pouts in her room. Apparently after Kane and I left the kitchen, Richard berated her for leaving the house without his permission. From what Kane told me it's a common occurrence. I don't see what the problem is. After all, Brooke is in her early twenties, but given how I found her in Requiem it's no wonder her father and brother are overprotective.

When I'm dry, I have to put on the same robe as I don't have any clothes except those I wore here yesterday morning. I knock on Brooke's door to check on her. She's curled up on the loveseat, her cheeks soaked in tears.

"I'm sorry," I say upon entering, closing the door behind me. "I heard what happened."

"And those two assholes wonder why I rebel," she says, fuming. "What was your life like growing up without your mother?"

"It was difficult," I reply, sitting on the side of her bed. "My dad took her death hard, then as the years passed without anyone being charged he began to drink. I fell by the wayside with every sip he took. I got into trouble in school, I was arrested a few times, but I had a couple of people help me through those rough spots, which is probably why I'm still alive and working at CSB."

"Who are they?"

"One is the detective in charge of my mother's case, and the other is my therapist. They both still look out for me to this day. It's almost like they're my surrogate parents, now that I think about it."

"Must be nice having people who care about you like that."

"I'm sure Richard and Kane mean well. They're just going about it all wrong."

"Maybe," she says, but she doesn't sound too sure. "Let's get ready for tonight."

After going through her closet, I settle on a gold sleeveless top that ties around my neck and is open in the back with only a thin hem at the bottom that barely covers my midriff. For pants I wear simple black, and Brooke loans me a pair of sandals. I retreat to Kane's room to dress, slip my phone into the back pocket just to have on hand, then return to Brooke's room to do my makeup and braid my hair. Once the two of us are all dolled up we head out to the covered lanai by the pool and sit at the bar in front of a small outdoor kitchen the caterers are using. We sip on fruity cocktails and gawk at the attractive servers as they setup tables.

Guests start arriving just after six with the first one being Joe. I let out a sigh of relief when I see him, which I hadn't realized I'd been holding. He gives me a perfunctory kiss on the cheek, and joins Brooke and I at the bar.

"How was it last night?" I ask.

"The girls in the pods made a killing," he says, smirking. "You would've earned thousands in tips if you worked the bar. It was insane the amount of people who came into the club after the fight. Security had their hands full."

"I'm surprised you came here alone."

"Tanner isn't feeling well, so I left him at home."

Tanner Jacobs has been Joe's partner for over twenty years. He owns an art gallery in Crer. He was a world-famous painter until arthritis crippled his hands, but instead of wallowing Joe insisted he open his own gallery to keep his passion alive. Tanner's paintings net millions at auction. He still tries to pick up a paintbrush every so often, but he can't turn out his gorgeous works like he once did.

"I hope it's nothing serious."

"He's just got a cold," Joe says, then chuckles. "He's such a big baby when it comes to being sick. He'll be fine in a few days."

Kane checks on us, but he can't stay as more people begin to arrive. The moment he's out of earshot Joe leans into me.

"Dean sent you more flowers this afternoon," he whispers. "He even tried to bribe his way into the club to see you, but my guards held him off. What did you do to him? He looks like a lost little puppy."

I tell Joe what transpired last night at the arena, the phone calls, and even the message Dean left last night.

"I take it you don't want to end the relationship with him," Joe comments.

"It's not a relationship," I utter, exasperated. "We're just friends. Fuck buddies as he put it so eloquently last week. At least that's what it used to be."

"You're going to need to tell him face-to-face that you've started dating Kane. It's the only way he'll get the message."

"I blame you for this," I say, jabbing my finger at him, teasing.

"I'll take full credit at the wedding." Joe grins before turning serious. "I saw all those boxes you have in the apartment. Are you working on something?"

"I'm helping Gail Rodgers with a few of her missing persons cases," I reply. "She thinks these particular ones are related, so I'm trying to determine how."

"I'd say they're from the same family," Joe snorts. "Those pictures you have hanging on the wall almost caused my heart to stop. The similarities between them is uncanny."

"I've told Gail to run a DNA analysis to see if there is, in fact, a familial match."

"Excuse me." Brooke abruptly darts toward the house.

I honestly forgot she was sitting there since my back had been toward her while I was speaking with Joe. A pit forms in my stomach as I fear she's made the connection between her and Erin like I did. I debate whether or not I should follow her when I catch sight of Dean walking out of the house with Luke Cobb beside him.

"Fuck," I utter, panic setting in.

Joe follows my eyeline. He takes my arm, pulling me off the barstool. "Follow me."

We go around the bar to another covered lanai along the other end of the family room, then enter the house through a side door. He places me at the wet bar in the kitchen, so I'm out of view of the windows.

"I need to find Kane," I say, becoming incensed.

"I'll get him. You stay here." Joe quickly leaves as I begin to shake.

I order a fresh drink from the bartender and have it almost finished by the time Kane arrives.

"Joe said you wanted to talk to me," he grunts, sounding put off.

"How the hell could you allow Dean in here?" I ask, gesturing towards the lanai, which I can't currently see. "Did you invite him or did Luke?"

"I invited him." Kane smiles, looking rather smug.

"Why would you do that considering what happened last night?"

"To show Dean I'm a reasonable man and to prove you're mine, not his."

"I'm not a possession, Kane." My tone rises along with my temper.

"Lower your voice," he demands. "Have another drink, Olivia. I'll be back after everyone has arrived."

When he's gone, I remove my cell and make my way into his bedroom. Bev's phone rings for several seconds before finally going to voicemail.

"Hi, Bev, it's Olivia. Look, I need your help. I may have placed myself into a situation I don't know how to get out of. Don't tell Frank since I don't need him swooping in to rescue me like the protective parent he tries to be. I just need advice. Please call me back as soon as you can."

I slip the phone back into my pocket before returning to the wet bar, but I don't order another drink for fear I might not be able to stop if I consume more alcohol. My nerves are rattled, my anxiety is over its limit, and I feel sick to my stomach.

"Excuse me, Ms. Darrow." Mabel taps me on the arm. "There's a gentleman waiting in the study to speak with you."

"Thank you," I respond, but I don't move right away as I need to get my trembling under control.

I head toward the foyer, which is crowded with guests still entering and being greeted by Kane and Richard. I slip past them without notice and step into the study on the other side. Dean is leaning against a large oak desk in the center of the room, glaring at me, his chest puffed out as he breathes heavily. I hesitate in closing the door to give us privacy, but I decide against my better judgement and do it.

"I thought I could trust you," he says, rage thick in his voice. "That maybe we could actually make it work this time."

"Dean—" I begin, but he waves his hand, causing me to shut up as hatred pulses in his irises.

"You told me the first time you met Kane Cassidy was the other night when you came to the arena to pick up Joe's tickets. You lied to me, Liv."

"No I didn't," I say, trying to sound firm. "That was the first time I met him."

"Stop lying!" he yells. "You're a fucking bitch, Olivia. You're just like your mother. Willing to fuck anyone no matter who it might hurt."

"What the hell are you talking about?" I ask, my anger growing.

He steps over to me, seizes my arm, and removes his phone from his pocket. The video is already queued up when he unlocks the screen, and he doesn't hesitate in hitting the play button. Displayed right before my eyes is the security feed Riddle recorded of Kane and I fucking in the hallway at Requiem. My legs begin to buckle, but Dean has a tight hold on me, preventing me from falling.

"Where…where did you get that?" I ask as I moan loudly on the video.

"It was sent to me by an unknown number," he replies, pausing the video and shoving me to the side. "How could you do this?"

"Me?" I ask, a resolve forming. "You're the one who pushed me into this situation. I told you I didn't want to be in a relationship, but you didn't give a damn what I had to say. You just kept shoving yourself further into my life, and I wasn't ready for it, so I reacted. I'm sorry you had to find out this way."

"No, you're only sorry because you got caught."

"How could someone have sent that footage to you? The only person who had access to it is in the detention center."

Dean sidles up beside me, his hot breath hitting me in the face. "Ask your boyfriend," he replies, then storms out of the room.

Kane wouldn't have access to the video… unless BluTrend owns Centurion. Frank said the company was a conglomeration, so it's possible the Cassidys, particularly Kane, control Centurion. It would also mean that Kane more than likely already knew his sister was hiding out at the club, but didn't tell his father. Yet he acted as if he wasn't aware she was there at all. Was this all a set up? But why? I feel like such a fool that I didn't put this together sooner.

It takes me a few minutes to gather myself together before I return to the foyer where Kane and Richard are still greeting people. I catch Kane's eye and seethe; his face falls. I make my way to his bedroom where I change into my clothes, making sure I have everything I brought with me as I have no intention of ever returning.

"Where the hell do you think you're going?" Kane demands, slamming the door behind him as he enters.

"I'm leaving." I sit on the side of the bed, putting on my shoes.

"No you're not." He snatches my purse. "You're not going anywhere."

"Fuck you, Kane," I say, my wrath growing. "I'm done with this bullshit."

"I saw Dean leave the study moments before you did. What happened in there? Did he say anything to you?"

"It wasn't anything he said, but what he showed me." I stand in preparation to leave. "Someone sent him the security recording of what happened between us at Requiem. How the hell could that have happened?" I don't want to acknowledge I know the truth as I want Kane to implicate himself in this nightmare.

"Because I asked the new manager at the club to send it to him," Kane states, an arrogant expression creasing his face.

"Why would you do that?" I ask, stunned.

"To get him to finally leave you alone."

"I can't believe you did that," I utter. "Who the hell do you think you are?"

"The man who loves you and can take care of you. You don't need scum like Robert Dean Morgan in your life. He wouldn't take the hint, so I had to hit him where I knew it would hurt. You're free now, Olivia. We can be together without any interference."

"That's not who I am, Kane." I rip my purse from his hands. "No one dictates who I can have in my life or even what I do with it. Not you or Dean. We're done, Kane. Don't ever contact me again."

I throw open the door, shove my way through the crowd to get out of the foyer into the warm evening air, and begin making my way along Wells. I'm halfway down Highland when I hear the engine of a car speeding up behind me. I move off to the side so I don't get hit, but the car slows and I recognize it as Joe's. He rolls down the window and tells me to get in, which I do.

"Were you intending on walking all the way back to the mainland?" he asks, driving toward the bridge.

"If I had to, yes."

"You left one hell of a shit storm back there. Dean is drinking himself into a coma and Kane has locked himself in the study for the time being. Where am I taking you? Home?"

"No, back to the club. I can't go home just yet since Dean has his things there. It's safer for me at the apartment."

"Do you want to tell me what happened?"

"Not particularly."

"If you change your mind I'm here to listen."

We ride the rest of the way in silence. After we enter the club, Joe changes the code on the security pad per my request since Kane knows it. He leaves as I head upstairs, finding the entire apartment littered with roses. I spend the next few hours tossing the bouquets and the ones Kane dropped on the floor into the dumpster out back, along with the candles, and scrub every surface as if trying to cleanse my soul. My stomach growls, so I eat some of the snack food I bought the other day, then brush my teeth and go to bed, but not before blocking Kane's number on my phone. I should delete it, but that doesn't prevent him from calling me. At least with his number blocked it'll make it a bit harder for him, but not impossible. I'll just have to block each number he might try to use if he does call, which I'm hoping he doesn't.

The following morning as I'm stepping out of the shower my cell begins to ring and I immediately tense up. Bev's name scrolls across the screen, causing me to relax.

"Where are you?" she asks. "I'm at your house, but no one is answering."

"I'm at Verdigris. Come in through the alley. I'm up on the top floor in the apartment in the front right corner."

"I'll bring breakfast," she says.

I give her the code to get inside as I don't want to leave the apartment today, if I can avoid it. After I dress, I sit down in front of the boxes belonging to Erin Carr and begin going through the notes Gail has on the case, hoping that if I throw myself back into work it'll help keep my mind off the mess that's now my life. She's written that Erin was a frequent patron of Temptation up until her disappearance, so it's consistent with what Brooke told me. Grabbing the notepad I'd starting using when I was going through Kelly Harris' files, I add a line for nightclubs, jotting down the dates Erin was supposedly there, which is easily verified by her microchip recording.

Out of curiosity, I go back to Kelly's Hub results, carefully reviewing the timeline when I notice something odd. Her family and friends said she wasn't into the club scene, yet there's at least one indication she went to Temptation only a few weeks before she disappeared. I add that to my list, including the date. The club shuttered two years ago, so I check the recordings for the third victim, a young woman named Catherine Lovell. She's been missing for just under three years, wasn't known to go clubbing, and like both Kelly and Erin she was at Temptation close to when she disappeared. I jot down her dates before picking up my laptop from the coffee table where I left it the other day. I have to plug it in as the battery is close to dying, then run a search on the dates under Temptation's archives, trying to find anything that might have drawn these women there.

When companies close, CSB takes possession of their internet domains as a way to maintain information in case we might need it. Nothing ever disappears entirely, except for maybe people.

Several flyers for a ladies' night appear on the screen, each one matching dates the three women were there. I rummage through the remaining two cases, finding their Hub recordings, only Temptation doesn't show on the results, Requiem does. I go back to my laptop and search their website, also finding a ladies' night on the days the last two victims were there. Reaching for my cell phone, which I placed on the floor by Erin's box, I call Frank.

"I heard you've had a very busy weekend," he says the minute he answers.

"I don't want to talk about that. I need you to find something out for me."

"What?"

"Who used to own Temptation."

"That's an easy one, Liv. Centurion controls that entire block. They ran the club until ERC forced them to shut it down."

"Have you been able to determine who owns Centurion?" I ask, hoping he has to confirm if my logic is correct.

"No as it's not a priority. Why? Is this related to what you're working on for Gail?"

"Yes. Is she in?"

"She's in a meeting right now, but I can have her call you the minute she's available."

"Have her do that." I hesitate in asking my next question. "Frank, what's happening with the Marsh case?"

"We've hit a wall," he answers, sounding downtrodden. "Foster has run out of leads, and unless we find something concrete, like where the poor girl was butchered, we can't charge anyone with the crime."

"And my father?"

"He's still a suspect, but he's not the only one. Focus on helping Gail and forget about the Marsh case. That's an order."

I hang up as there's a knock on my door; Bev stands on the other side with a bag of containers.

"I wasn't sure how hungry you were," she says, stepping inside. She places the bag on the counter and unloads the food as her gaze wanders over to the boxes and photographs. "Frank told me you were helping Detective Rodgers. Have you discovered anything?"

"I might have, but I'm waiting to hear back from Gail before I make any more assumptions."

Bev scrunches up her face as I set out plastic utensils that came with our food. "You're hiding something, Olivia," she says. "Does it have anything to do with the message you left me?"

"Yes, and no." I tell her what transpired at the arena and the estate, not leaving out a single detail about either Dean or Kane's behavior. I also divulge my theory that Kane owns Centurion and the possibility that I was setup in locating his sister.

"I can see why you would be concerned. It sounds like Kane might be a narcissist if he's dictating everything about your life. Especially if what you feel about being hired to find his sister is true. I'm sure he learned it from his father since Richard is known for his demanding behavior and his need to be valued above all others. But there's more to it, isn't there?"

"When I was at the estate this weekend I found a picture of one of the missing women among a collage Brooke has in her room," I explain, gesturing towards Erin's photo. "The two looked almost identical. Brooke said Erin was one of her club friends and the two were often mistaken as sisters."

"And you believe the women *are* related," Bev states, finishing my thought. "Do you think Richard might be the father of at least this one young woman?"

"Yes. I told Gail to run a familial profile on the five cases she gave me to see if any match."

"Then it's your belief Richard fathered all these women."

"It's quite possible. Did you know my mother was his secretary?"

"No," Bev answers, shocked. "That I wasn't aware of. Who told you?"

"Richard did when he was driving us to the arena."

"Your mother was pregnant when she died. Is it possible that in the back of your mind you now suspect the child she was carrying could've been Richard Cassidy's?"

I don't want to admit that's exactly what I'm thinking, so instead of answering I focus on eating.

"I'll take that as a yes," Bev says.

My cell phone rings, Gail's name scrolling across the screen.

"What's up?" she asks after I answer.

"I might have found another connection between your victims."

"What is it?"

"They all visited either the clubs Temptation or Requiem shortly before disappearing, and both are owned by a company called Centurion."

"At least three of those women were not into the club scene. Why would they have gone?"

"The dates on their Hub recordings match with a ladies' night event happening at these places. I think they may have been lured there out of pretext."

"By whom?"

"I haven't figured that part out yet," I reply, lying. "Did you run the DNA?"

"Hayden's team is working on that now, but it'll take time. Let me know if you find anything else. I'll check out Centurion."

"You didn't tell her," Bev says after I end the call.

"I can't afford to be wrong about this."

"And if you're right?"

"I want Gail to figure this out. If I do, it might be misconstrued. The chief may see it as me trying to get revenge for what Kane did to me with sending that damning video to Dean. The evidence would be thrown out, and Kane, or his father, will get away with everything. I can only lay the breadcrumbs. Gail has to follow them and put the puzzle together."

"How long are you going to hang out here?"

"At least until tomorrow. I don't want to run into Dean when he comes to collect his belongings."

"If you could do things over, would you?"

"You mean sleeping with Kane? I honestly don't know. Somehow I get the feeling I would've found myself in this predicament no matter what choices I made."

"What do you want next out of life?"

"To get back to work and put this entire mess behind me."

"I'll tell Frank to place you on active duty. It'll be a good distraction for you."

I smile, then we clean up the containers and Bev leaves a short time later. Returning to the boxes, I start with Erin's and review the photos taken of her apartment since she lived alone. Nothing appears out of place—there's no sign of a struggle—and her purse is sitting nice and neat on the table by the front door along with her car keys. Her bed is made, empty laundry baskets are piled in the corner of her bedroom, and the top of her dresser has personal items such as photos, earrings, necklaces, and an empty jewelry box.

A lightbulb goes off in the back of my mind.

Kelly Harris had a jewelry box listed on the inventory sheet for her car, but there isn't a picture of it in her files. I move over to Catherine Lovell's, paying close attention to not only the photos, but the inventory sheets from her car. Pictured in the kitchen is a simple white jewelry box, open, with a light blue ribbon draped along its side. I check the other two victims and find the same. I look over the one from Catherine's case as it has the closest shot.

The box is nondescript; plain and simple. There aren't any embellishments along its smooth, flat surface and it doesn't appear a card came with the item, so there's no way to trace who sent it or where it came from. The box is empty, as are all the others, so maybe the women were wearing the item when they disappeared. I should call Gail and tell her about this, but she's already got plenty on her plate with the information I've given her. Putting my shoes on, I take the photo along with my purse, and head down to the alley. There's dozens of jewelry stores in Crer alone, but Range has a few, and since all of the women lived in that sector I decide to start there first.

I spend several hours traveling through the area stopping at every jewelry store I come across and none use a plain, white box. Several proprietors advise me that type of box can be purchased at any store, which only adds to my frustrations. My stomach growls, so I go against my better judgement and swing by my house to grab a quick bite. After parking the Nimbus in the back driveway, I go to open the garage door from the dashboard and I'm alerted that the alarm to the house was deactivated earlier this morning and is still off.

"Great," I grumble. "The least you could've done was reset the alarm after you got your shit, Dean."

I enter through the door in the garage, proceeding cautiously into the house. Dean's boxes are still sitting by the bedroom door, and when I step into the room his clothes are piled on the floor. Going back to the living room, I turn on my television, and call up the recording from this morning to see who entered my home. Nothing but static fills the screen. I switch to different cameras and all have the same interference. Exiting out of the recordings, I go to a live feed. Again, I'm met with static.

"What the hell?"

I step over to my desk where the main panel is kept and freeze. Sitting on my desk is a white jewelry box with a light blue ribbon tied neatly around it. I slowly set my purse down and reach inside to retrieve my gun when something hard is pressed against the side of my head.

"I wouldn't do that if I were you," Riddle says, shoving the barrel of his gun into my temple.

"How'd you get out of the detention center?" I ask, fear gripping me.

"It helps to know the right people," he hisses. "And I know a lot of people."

"How did you get into my house?"

"That's a little secret I intend on keeping to myself, love. Now, be a good girl and open your present." He nods toward the box.

When I don't do it, he presses the gun harder into my head. "Do it," he demands. "Or there won't be a brain left in that beautiful head of yours."

With trembling fingers I gently pull on the ribbon, loosening its bow until it falls away, then slowly lift the lid. Inside is a thin, silver bracelet nestled on top of a piece of cotton. There isn't a note or anything else identifying where it came from.

"Put it on," Riddle orders.

"Why should I?"

"So I don't have to put a bullet through your brain."

I glare at him, not budging.

"I knew you were going to make this difficult."

He punches me in the head after lowering his weapon. Stunned, I fall to the floor, the world spinning around me. I feel him on top of me, pinning me down as I try to fight him off the best I can. He slips the bracelet on and I feel an immediate painful surge of power course through my right arm. I scream in agony until Riddle takes the butt of his gun, striking me across the head again, this time knocking me out.

Ten

The pain behind my eyes is intense and the harshness from the light in the ceiling isn't helping. I groan as my stomach turns with every motion no matter how miniscule. The mattress I'm lying on is thin, allowing the springs of the bed to poke me in the side. My arms are stretched above my head, handcuffed around the thin, metal frame. The room is small, stuffy, and contains only one other piece of furniture—a couch where Riddle is sitting and grinning as he twirls a hunting knife in his hands. His gun rests on the cushion beside him.

"Where am I?" I ask, which only causes more pain and discomfort.

"My favorite night spot."

"Requiem."

"Very good, love."

"Why'd you bring me here?"

"Because I was told to," he says, standing.

"By whom?" I ask, even though I already know the answer.

"Now, see, that's where it gets tricky." He kneels beside me, his face close to mine, his foul breath stinging my eyes. "I'm not sure who wants your ass in a sling other than me. I simply follow orders when they're given, and I don't particularly care by who as long as I get paid. I was only told to make sure you wore your glorious gift and to bring you here by any means necessary. You'll be collected shortly, but before then I have some payback to give you." He points to the group of stitches on his face where my heel went through his cheek.

Removing a wad of cloth from this back pocket, he shoves it in my mouth, then digs the tip of his knife into my skin, dragging it down my arm, opening my flesh. I scream as best I can, but the cloth is muffling my sounds. Tears stream down my face as he starts again, making another cut beside the first one. Blood soaks the bed as well as my clothes. Riddle grins at my pain before opening a door by the head of the bed, disappearing from view. Even though I'm in agony,

I try to see if there's a way to free myself from the handcuffs. I pull and twist my hands, digging the metal into my wrists, bruising them.

"I thought CSB detectives were smarter than you," Riddle says upon his return, closing the door behind him. "Apparently they're dumber than I thought. Here, I brought you a little something."

He kneels beside me, brandishing a small syringe filled with a clear liquid.

"No," I try to cry, but the gag in my mouth makes it difficult.

I push myself as far back on the bed as possible, but it's not out of his reach. Riddle laughs as he drives the needle into my bicep. Within minutes my vision begins to wane, my hearing becomes muffled, and everything around me looks as if it's in slow motion. Riddle's smile blurs as his figure becomes a simple blob. I blink to clear my vision, which helps, but only briefly. Riddle climbs on top of me, groping me as his mouth sucks on my neck.

"The things I can do to you," he whispers. "I better hurry before we're interrupted."

I hear something crack, which causes Riddle to jump to his feet. Flashes cross my field of vision, but the noise is muted. Riddle stumbles back, collapsing against the couch as his shirt soaks with blood. I close my eyes as I feel the gag being removed and my hands freed.

"I've got you," a contorted voice whispers in my ear, but in my condition I don't know who it belongs to.

I'm lifted off the bed, and while I'm being carried through the maze of hallways I try to focus on the person holding me, but it becomes too much and I eventually pass out.

My whole-body hurts and I'm dreading where I might be. I carefully open my eyes, taking in the subdued light. Sconces embedded in the wall are dim, casting odd shadows around the room. The bed I'm on is queen-sized with soft sheets, firm pillows, and a warm blanket. The walls are painted a light blue, and the only decoration is a large television behind glass encased in the far wall. There aren't any windows and only one door. I slowly sit up, being overly cautious due to how I feel, and swing my feet out of the bed. Plush carpeting covers the floor, and I nearly sink when I touch it. I look over at my left arm, which is heavily bandaged from my shoulder to my wrist, but I can't feel any pain from the deep cuts, though I ache all over. The bracelet that had been on my right wrist is gone, as are my shoes and socks.

I feel disoriented and confused, which is only made worse when I try to stand, promptly falling back onto the bed. Taking a deep breath, I force myself to my feet, and immediately collapse to the floor. It takes me a few seconds before I manage to crawl over to the door and try the handle, which is locked. Propping myself against the wall, I wait, not only because I can't think straight, but because I'm nauseous as hell. There isn't anything I can do at the moment, and my brain isn't firing on all cylinders to make a comprehensive plan of an escape. I'm not sure how much time passes before the television turns on, drawing my attention. It takes a lot of effort for me to focus on the display. I want to be shocked by what I see, but I'm not, and it sickens me.

"What is she doing here?" Brooke raves at Kane as the two stand in the living room.

"Riddle didn't give me much of a choice," Kane counters. "That fucking boyfriend of yours was only supposed to hold her for a few days to throw off suspicion that she might be with us, but he was out of control, nearly killing her with those drugs. He cut her arm up pretty bad and was in the midst of raping her when I stormed in since I'd caught him on the security cameras. I had to stop him and bring her here so her wounds could be taken care of, otherwise they would've gotten infected if I'd left her in that rat trap."

"Well you're the idiot who told him to get her," Brooke says, shoving Kane. "It's your own damn fault. You put her in that situation knowing full well the animosity Riddle had for her. But no, you just couldn't leave well enough alone, could you? Olivia had to be the one. Thank God she's one we're looking for. End her life already. Get it over with so we can move on from this nightmare."

"She's not one of them," Kane says, clenching his teeth. "This situation is different from the others."

"Why? Because you love her?"

"Because she's not one of his!" Kane shouts.

"What?" Brooke asks, genuinely shocked. "Olivia isn't Richard's?"

"No, you stupid cunt. I only told you that so you'd go along with the ruse." Kane turns melancholy, as if reliving a wonderful memory. "I've wanted Olivia for months now, ever since I saw her at Verdigris when Luke took me there to discuss scheduling the fight. I knew who she was, the work she did for our father's friends, and I was desperate to make her mine, so I did a little research discovering her mother worked for Richard right up until she was murdered. Everything fell into place after that. It was perfect."

"Until Dean interfered."

"I should've killed that asshole when I had the chance. It would've been easy, too, given his propensity for violence. All he'd need to do is piss off the wrong guy and it would be over within a matter of moments. I wasn't counting on Olivia's attachment to him or how eager Dean was to keep her as his own."

"Do you love her?"

"Yes, I love her. Why do you think I went to such extremes? I didn't do this for pure enjoyment."

"Yes you did, Kane. It just added an additional arousal factor that you're attracted to her. I'm surprised at how subdued your chase was. I thought for sure you would've made it more dramatic, knowing your ego."

"I couldn't do that to Olivia. She required time. I had to get it just right."

"You still wound up fucking everything up. Richard is going to be furious when he finds out what you've done. He's not going to let you keep her… let alone keep her alive."

"I don't give a damn what he thinks. He'll only know she's here if you tell him. So if you value your life in any way you'll keep your damn mouth shut."

"What about Mabel? She saw you bring Olivia in here. She's the one who took care of her wounds."

"Mabel knows better than to say anything. Otherwise I'll implicate her as an accomplice."

"You don't think CSB is going to notice one of their homicide detectives is missing? You can only keep her hidden for so long before hell rains down on us," Brooke says, scared. "She recognized Erin's picture, for God's sake. You told me she had the files of the missing women in the apartment above Verdigris. Fuck, Kane. Olivia may have figured it all out and told her superiors. What if she told Detective Rodgers what she's discovered? We're screwed, and all because you fell for someone you shouldn't have."

"All the more reason to keep her here," Kane says, rubbing Brooke's arms. "It'll be fine. I can handle whatever Olivia thinks she's discovered and manipulate the rest with the technology we have at the company. Besides, she was wearing one of my bracelets when I picked her up from Requiem. No one will know she's missing for at least a few days, and even then their precious Hub won't be able to locate her."

I lift my right arm, my finger rubbing over the area where my microchip lies. I see the pieces falling into place, but my mind is too muddled from the drugs for it to completely sink in.

"Olivia can't stay down there forever. That room isn't equipped to keep someone prisoner for more than a day or two. Especially if you don't intend on killing her."

"I'll figure it out," he says, releasing her. "She should be awake by now. Don't say anything to anyone or you'll be dead like your boyfriend." He jabs a finger in Brooke's face, then the television shuts off.

I simply sit there, staring at the blank screen as my mind is too clouded to process everything all at once. I try to separate the information into manageable segments, but it's still all garbled. I wish I knew what Riddle gave me so I'd know how much longer I'm going to feel this way.

The lock on the door gives with Kane slowly entering. It takes him a few seconds to find me sitting on the floor by the door, which he closes before kneeling beside me.

"Why?" I stammer.

"Why what, my love?" he asks, stroking my cheek.

"Riddle," I say, then point toward the television.

"Oh, you want to know why I had Riddle come to your house?"

I nod.

"So I could bring you here for safe keeping," Kane responds. "I couldn't go to your place myself as it would look suspicious. I gave Riddle the equipment he'd need to disable your alarm, and according to the detention's records he's still locked in his cell. At least that's what the Hub will see if they look at his microchip recordings." He pushes an errant hair behind my ear. "CSB relies too much on technology BluTrend creates, which they believe is infallible. Gone are the days of using one's own senses to tell you what's real. It's dumbed down society enough that people can get away with everything nowadays."

I go to open my mouth, but I can't formulate anything to say.

"That asshole did a number on you," Kane says, sounding concerned. "Well, he can't hurt you any longer. Let me help you back into bed." Placing his hands under my arms, Kane lifts me up, then settles me on the mattress, sliding in beside me. He starts to tug on my clothes as his lips brush against mine. "I should let you rest because of everything you've been through, but I just can't help myself when you're within reach." He kisses me hard, his hands wandering my body as he undresses me. It's not long until he slips inside, his moans filling the room. "I need you so much, Olivia. Damn it feels good to be with you."

He thrusts himself deep, sighing heavily with each motion before finally shuttering as he climaxes. His mouth travels down my body, his tongue penetrating me between the legs as he bends my knees, practically shoving my legs over my head. He sucks on my clitoris until I come, which doesn't take long. I let out an involuntary cry as I soak the bed, which satisfies him. He pulls the sheets over our sweat-drenched bodies, wrapping me in his arms.

"I love you, Olivia," he whispers. "We're going to be so happy together."

I simply lie there feeling dead to the world, praying my brain returns to normal soon so I don't have to endure Kane's abuse and control for too long. Eventually my eyelids close and I fall asleep.

When I wake Kane is gone and I'm neatly tucked under the blanket wearing a silk nightgown. Without any windows I don't know what time of day it is. I no longer feel muddle-headed and the bandages have been removed from my arm leaving me with scars which are in the process of healing. They'll be constant reminders of the torture Riddle imposed on me before my supposed rescuer stepped in to save the day. The door to the room opens, and Kane enters holding a breakfast tray, which he sets across my lap after forcing me to sit up.

"I was starting to worry," he says, then kisses me. "I thought I was going to have to send for a doctor."

"What day is it?"

"Thursday."

"I've been unconscious for three days?"

"Riddle gave you a decent dose of ketamine. That shit can knock you out for a long time, which also means you haven't eaten so you need food." Kane gestures toward the tray.

My stomach growls at the smell of freshly cooked eggs and buttered toast, but I know better than to eat it. "How long do you plan on keeping me down here?"

"Until I can trust you not to run off or call for help."

"So I'm here until I die."

"It doesn't have to be that way if you simply do as you're told, listen to me implicitly, and never leave my side," he says, sitting beside me. "We can have a great life together, Olivia. I'm not as horrible as you believe me to be. You just need to give us a chance and you'll see that I'm right."

"Go fuck yourself, Kane." I toss the tray onto the floor.

He slaps me hard, cutting my lip, then pulls out a pair of handcuffs from his pocket, pins me to the bed, and secures one of my wrists to a ring in the wall just above my head. I know that wasn't there before… at least I don't think it was. My memory from the first night, or day, I was here is still blurry. I recall snippets of the things I heard him discuss with Brooke, but they're sluggish in reaching the surface.

Kane steps out of the room, returning sometime later with Mabel, who cleans up the mess. The woman won't even acknowledge I'm there. She keeps her head down, does her job, and quickly leaves.

"If you don't want to eat, that's fine," Kane grouses the minute the door is closed. "I have no problem starving you until I get what I want."

"Is this what you did with the other women? Held them hostage because they refused your advances?"

Kane laughs. "No, Olivia. They were dead less than a day after vanishing," he says with ease, sitting on the side of the bed. "And I wasn't keeping them against their will. Many didn't even wake up after Riddle immobilized them with the ketamine."

"Then why did you kidnap them?"

"To clean up my father's mess, of course. We couldn't very well have heirs to his immense fortune other than Brooke and me. Although I'm not thrilled with the idea of having to share it with her either. Richard's bastard children needed to be dealt with before they realized the legacy they were entitled to."

"But they didn't even know. You couldn't have foreseen them ever finding out."

"*I knew*, and that's all that mattered," he says, irate.

"What about me? I'm not one of his children."

"I know, since the child he placed in your family died when your mother did. And before you ask, I didn't kill her. I wasn't made

164

aware of my father's many indiscretions until five years ago when he confessed it to me during a night of drunken revelry. The bastard finally got himself a vasectomy after Brooke was born, leaving only a few offspring for me to hunt."

"That still doesn't explain why I'm here."

"You already know why you're here, love. I can't live without you." He leans forward, kissing me hard. "I told you I'd do anything to make sure you stayed mine and I did just that." He lies on top of me and removes my nightgown as best he can while his mouth continues to devour mine.

"Only it backfired," I say, smirking when he moves to nuzzle my neck.

"I hadn't counted on you turning on me like you did after I sent Dean the recording," Kane says, his temper rising as his gaze bores into mine. "My hope was that once he saw that the two of us had been together in such an intimate, open, and exquisite way, he'd break it off with you for good. Which he did, only you became resentful toward me instead of grateful for ridding your life of that trash." Kane places his hand on my cheek. "He didn't deserve you. No one does, except me. I just wish you saw it before now."

"Dean may be an asshole, but he'd never force himself on me like you're doing."

"How soon we forget," Kane says, chuckling. "He was doing that very thing when I came along. You told me over and over again how he was pushing you into a relationship you didn't want any part of." Kane shoves the covers off and begins to disrobe.

"Isn't that exactly what you're doing?"

"No, as I'm simply opening your eyes to the kind of life I can offer." Kane shoves himself inside of me. "I have the ability to free you from working in Nok and even from CSB with the amount of money and prestige I carry."

He kisses my neck, then his mouth moves to my breasts where he begins to suckle. He returns to kissing me as I feel myself coming, though I don't want to. I moan as the muscles between my legs seize him, causing him to orgasm. Kane practically hollers as he comes, drenching me and the bed.

"Fuck, Olivia," he utters. "This is how our life should always be. You can have anything and everything you've ever wanted, and I'll happily give it to you. Your father will never be able to bother you again as he'll be prohibited from stepping foot on the island. We'll have several children and I'd never stray from you like my father did to his wives. You'd never have cause to cheat on me like your mother did to your father. I'd be implicitly yours, and you mine. Our happiness will rival others and you'll never have to want ever again."

"You live in a fairytale, Kane," I say, my heart beating rapidly. "Life for regular people is never so easy. Anything you want to provide me will come with consequences, like my freedom or the ability to think for myself. You just want someone in your life you can control and do everything you ask without question. That's not who I am or who I want to be."

"Which is why you're here," he says. "So I can show you what our life together will be like, and it's not the monstrous ideas you're flinging around. I love you like no one else will ever be able to. I'm never going to let you go, Olivia, so you might as well give in."

"Was this always going to be the outcome in your eyes? That I'd throw myself at you, grateful you freed me from a horrible existence?"

"Yes, but when it failed I had to act quickly as I couldn't chance losing you. Which is why I sent Riddle first to Verdigris then to your house."

"What are you going to do when I don't come around to your way of thinking? Because I won't."

He strokes my cheek. "You will, Olivia. Just give it time."

"Kane," Brooke calls through the television as it flips on, her eyes wide with fear. "There are two detectives at the front door."

"Who?"

"Detectives Foster and Corro from homicide."

"I'll be up in a minute. Keep them outside on the lanai and turn on that camera so Olivia can watch." Kane dresses and kisses me before heading for the door.

"The bracelet, it disables the microchip, doesn't it?" I inquire before he steps out of the room.

"It kills it, actually. Making it permanently useless."

He closes and locks the door as the camera for the covered lanai turns on showing Brooke gesture for Gabe and Frank to have a seat on the barstools for the outside kitchen, but only Gabe takes her up on the offer. They're joined a few minutes later by Kane, who shakes Gabe's hand then stands off to the side, making sure I have an unobstructed view. Frank keeps his hands clasped together, his eyes narrowed on Kane, carefully studying him, while standing slightly off to the side of the group.

"What can I assist you with, detectives?" Kane asks, his voice calm and even.

"When was the last time you were in contact with Olivia Darrow?" Gabe inquires as Frank remains silent.

"I saw her Sunday. She was here at the house for an after party my father and I were hosting. She got into an argument with one of the guests and left. I haven't seen or spoken to her since."

"Who was the guest she argued with?"

"Robert Dean Morgan. He works for Luke Cobb and accompanied him to the party."

"Why doesn't that surprise me?" Gabe utters, glancing at Frank, who's unmoved by the comment.

It's not a secret among CSB about the tumultuous relationship Dean and I have as we were constantly in each other's face when working, which is what made the sex so great. We could take our animosity out in the bedroom and never fail to surprise each other with the things we'd try or do.

"How long did Dean stay after Olivia left?" Gabe asks, pulling me out of a pleasant memory.

"He was here until midnight, then Luke took him home from my understanding. You'd have to ask either of them, though, to be certain."

"What about you, Brooke? Have you been in contact with Ms. Darrow?" Gabe asks.

I'm surprised Frank isn't conducting the interviews since he's our supervisor. Perhaps he's studying Brooke and Kane's reactions, trying to determine what might be lies mixed in with the truth.

"No," Brooke replies, with only the slightest bit of anxiety showing. "I saw her here at the party, but not since."

"When was the last time you were at Requiem?"

"Last week," Brooke replies.

"Did either of you know Carter Byrne? He also went by the club name of Riddle."

"He and I used to date," Brooke answers. "He used to manage Requiem until he was arrested. Is he still in the detention center?"

"It seems he managed to slip out sometime over the weekend, but we haven't been able to figure out how," Gabe responds. "We believe he may have gone looking for Ms. Darrow because of what occurred at the club last week when you were recovered." Gabe points to Brooke with his comment.

"What's this all about?" Kane crosses his arms over his chest.

"Riddle's body was found in a back room in Requiem when the manager arrived to open for the night on Monday," Gabe replies. "The same room you were found in, Brooke."

"What does this have to do with Olivia?" His expression turning to one of concern.

"While Riddle was in the detention center he bragged about going after Detective Darrow for mangling his face and ruining his opportunity for making quick money," Gabe replies. "The guy had a short fuse, and she must have set him off in the worst possible way. Now he's dead and she's missing."

"Olivia's missing?" Kane's hands falling to his sides as his mouth hangs open. "What are you doing to find her?"

"Everything we can, Kane," Gabe says, trying to settle him down while Frank continues to monitor the scene. "We believe whoever killed Riddle has Olivia, or at least knows where she is… if she's still alive."

"What?" Kane begins to choke on crocodile tears.

"Her blood was found on a mattress in the room where Riddle was discovered. We located a bloody knife in the manager's office, and the blood matched Olivia."

The only reason Gabe is disclosing this information is if Frank told him to. Otherwise, if it wasn't Frank's idea he would've stopped the questioning before it got to this point. Frank's playing a mind game and he's using Gabe to conduct the test.

"What can I do to help? You can have anything you need from BluTrend to aid in the search." Kane is shaking as the tears continue to pour. "You have to find her, Detective Foster. Olivia means the world to me."

"I heard the two of you started dating," Gabe says. "But you haven't spoken or seen her since Sunday?"

"I've been busy closing out business with the vendors from Saturday's fight. I left her several voice and text messages, so I just assumed she was busy with work which is why she hasn't called me back. I drove by her house a few times to see if she was home, but she never answered the door and her car wasn't in the driveway, though it might have been in the garage, for all I know."

Kane's never been to my house, at least not to my knowledge. He'd have no way of knowing I have two driveways and that the Nimbus was parked in the one at the rear of the house when Riddle kidnapped me. Unless he took it to transport me between my home and Requiem. That's easy to trace. I gauge Frank's reaction to the slip, only he has a damn good poker face so I can't tell if he's realized Kane's mistake or not.

Gabe's cell phone begins to ring. He excuses himself to answer it, returning a few minutes later after getting off the call. Frank remains silent, his face hard as stone making only Brooke uncomfortable.

169

Kane glares at my boss, causing Frank to grow angrier as his knuckles turn white from gripping his hands tighter together.

"Kane, did you and Olivia have a fight Sunday night?" Gabe asks, reclaiming his seat.

"It was just a misunderstanding."

"According to her boss, Joe Ambrose, it was more than a simple misunderstanding. She broke up with you that night, didn't she?"

"Is that what he told you?" Kane asks, surprised.

"That's what she said to him when he drove her home that night since she didn't have a way off the island after leaving your house."

"Then he's missing the second half of the story," Kane says. "Joe didn't take her home, but back to Verdigris where she's been staying since last week Thursday. She let me into the building and we talked in her apartment well into the night. It took some time, but we worked things out and agreed to keep seeing each other."

"According to the Hub, Olivia's last known location was her home in Range, not the club," Gabe says. "When we entered her house we found her purse with her cell phone in it and she had your number blocked. Any idea why she would've done that if the two of you had reconciled?"

"No," he answers, perplexed.

"Do either of you know anyone who would want to hurt Detective Darrow?"

"Besides Dean, and now obviously Riddle?" Kane asks. "I'm not aware of anyone else."

Frank nudges Gabe, signaling it's time to leave.

"Well, if either of you can think of anything give me a call," Gabe says, standing, then reaches into his pocket to extract one of his business cards, handing it to Kane.

Brooke shows them to the door as the television shuts off. It's not long before Kane returns, a smile plastered across his face.

"That was close," he says.

"How did you know Joe took me back to Verdigris?"

"Because I followed him. I sat in my car watching the place until well after midnight, then came home. It wasn't until Riddle tried the code on the alley door a few hours later did I know it had been changed, which is why I sent him to your house in the off chance you'd go there—or Dean would, in which case Riddle was to kill him. Lucky for your boyfriend you got there first."

"Now what?"

"I'll take you upstairs in a few minutes to shower and get some food into you, then it's back down here unless you're willing to concede."

"No way in hell," I growl.

"Have it your way."

He steps from the room, leaving the door partially open. I hear his footsteps receding up what sounds to be a wooden staircase, a door squeaking open a few seconds later. He comes back with a handgun and a set of small keys, which he tosses to me.

"Uncuff yourself, but try anything and I will shoot you."

I'm not afraid of having a gun pointed at me since this isn't the first time. However, on previous occasions I either had backup or my weapon on hand. I have neither at the moment, and with me being declared a missing person Kane has the upper hand. He can easily kill me and discard my body like he did with those other women and I'd be lost forever. Another unsolved case like my mother's.

I unlock my wrist, leaving the other cuff attached to the ring in the wall, then hand the keys back to him. I'm now able to ascertain how the ring is adhered as I slowly adjust my nightgown since it's still over my head.

Some type of anchor has been drilled into the wall, probably into the stud, then the ring appears to be attached like a picture hook. I'm sure with enough movement and force I might be able to loosen the nail enough to slide the ring out of the anchor. But I'd need to time it carefully as I'm sure Kane has other means of keeping me hostage if this one fails and I don't want to find out what those might be.

Grasping my arm, Kane shoves the muzzle of the gun into my side, then escorts me out of the room and into a narrow hallway with

171

a lone staircase at the far end. When we reach the top, one of the bookcases in the study has been pushed forward, allowing us entry. Kane leaves it open as we make our way into his bathroom. I stand in the corner while he draws a bath, then remove the nightgown and step into the hot water with him joining me. He rests the gun on the tile floor, but out of my reach. I sit there while he washes me, thinking of ways to get myself out of this prison.

After we've dried and I'm wearing cotton shorts with a matching top, Kane leads me into the kitchen where Mabel has dinner waiting for us. He rests the gun on the table, still aimed at me while we eat. I glare at him with each bite, detesting everything I ever allowed to happen between us. Mabel clears our plates as Kane takes me back to my cell where I'm secured to the wall once again. I wait for him to jump into bed with me, but he simply kisses me on the forehead then leaves, locking the door behind him. As I lie in the dark I take the chance and slowly begin tugging on the ring, only it's not budging and my wrist starts to hurt after a few minutes. I don't give up and keep at it until I hear someone approaching the room. Kane enters, but doesn't bother turning on the light. He closes the door, crawls into bed, and fucks me until he passes out from exhaustion.

Eleven

Muffled shouts can be heard overhead, followed by the pounding of heavy feet. A door squeals as if it's being violently opened, then the door to the bedroom flies open, Richard filling the doorframe. He flips on the light switch, and I try to cover myself with the blanket as best I can since Kane stripped me of my clothes when he came to bed.

"So, she is here," Richard says, simmering. "I should've known when that damn detective showed up at the company. Do you know the jeopardy you've placed this family in?"

"No more than you have," Kane counters, getting to his feet after putting on his pajama bottoms.

"This isn't some random woman you can easily dispose of, Kane. She's a God damn detective," Richard says, his face reddening. "The entire bureau is out searching for her, and they will eventually find her. Kill her and be done with it. Bury her in the rose garden with the others."

My mouth falls open. The area between the garage and the study has dozens of rose bushes filling the immense space. That has to be the spot Richard is referring to. Kane must have placed his victims there so he could easily marvel at his control over those women's lives even in death.

"No," Kane says, fuming. "Olivia lives. She's not like the others. She's not yours."

"Don't you think I know that?" Richard snorts. "It doesn't matter. Olivia has to die. She knows too much, and there's no way in hell she's going to keep her mouth shut. Murder the bitch already so we can move on with our lives."

"You knew he killed those women this whole time?" I ask, stunned.

"Who do you think gave him the idea?" Richard smirks. "I know what my son is. His obsessive behavior, his thirst for power and control. I used it to my advantage by convincing him the threat those women were to his wellbeing, his fortune, and his place in society. He killed them because I instructed him to do so. However, you were never part of the equation. It was a mistake hiring you to locate Brooke. I should've gone another route."

"Did Kane convince you to hire me?" I ask.

"Come to think of it, he did," Richard says, stroking his chin. "He was rather insistent about it, too."

"That's because he set the both of us up," I say, glaring at Kane as he scowls. "Brooke wasn't missing. Kane knew exactly where she was because he placed her at Requiem and probably paid Riddle to keep her doped up so she couldn't leave until the time was right. It was all a trap, a setup against the both of us. The first to lure me into trusting and falling for him, so when the time came he thought I'd simply follow along as I'm sure most of his girlfriends have done. What I haven't figured out, though, is why he'd set you up?"

"That's why," Kane says, nodding.

Richard turns, and we both notice Brooke standing in the hallway, a gun held firmly in her gloved hands. I immediately recognize it as my CSB issued weapon, which was left behind in my house—unless Riddle took it when he brought me to Requiem. Brooke fires without hesitation, hitting Richard in the chest multiple times. He crumples to the floor, his face forever frozen in terror.

"Get the car ready, Brooke. I'll be up in a few minutes."

Smiling, she leaves.

"What are you going to do?" I ask, genuinely frightened.

"You'll see," he replies, grinning.

"They're going to know I didn't shoot that weapon since my fingerprints won't be on it, and that your father's life ended here when they run his Hub recording. Whatever you're planning, it's not going to work."

"That's where you're wrong, Olivia. I'd love to go into greater detail, but my time is short."

He kisses me, then hurries from the room. It's not long before he returns wearing overalls and carrying a thick, hefty bag. Mabel joins

174

him, and the two shove Richard's body into the plastic before hauling it upstairs. She comes back a minute or so later carrying a television remote, which seems odd to me.

"In case you get bored while we're gone." She tosses it onto the bed, then proceeds to shut the door, making sure to lock it but leaving the light on.

After dressing, I start to work on loosening the anchor from the wall. The metal of the cuff digs sharply into my wrist and I wind up cutting myself, but not deeply. I change my position so I'm kneeling on my pillow to get a closer look at the device.

A metal plate drilled into the wall rests just under the surface of several layers of paint, which the ring is anchored to. When I initially glanced at the attachment I thought it was a simple picture hook type assembly, but now seeing it up close a pit forms in my stomach as it won't be as easy to free myself as I was hoping. I spot paint flaking from the plate, exposing a few areas speckled in red making me wonder if the others tried to free themselves like I'm doing. It wouldn't surprise me if this room has been painted over several times as blood is difficult to get out of sheetrock. Peeling part of the paint away, I reveal a multitude of colors. I continue to shred what I can from around the plate, exposing the rest of the metal. I know Kane will notice, but there isn't much I can do about that. The only way I'll be able to get this loose is by chiseling away the drywall and praying the bolts aren't too deep into the stud. If I get an opportunity, I'll try to swipe a knife from the kitchen, though I'm sure that'll be impossible to accomplish.

Exacerbated for the moment I sit down and use the remote to turn on the television, but the only thing airing are old talk shows, which is normal during the late-night hours. Shutting it off, I drop the remote on the floor, and wrap myself in the blanket as I try to work on other plans of escape

I must have fallen asleep as the light in the room is now off. Kane is lying beside me, staring at me.

"Good morning, beautiful." He brushes the hair out of my eyes.

"What did you do with Richard's body?" I ask, trembling.

"You'll find out soon enough."

"He's right, you know. You can't keep me here forever."

"That's where you're both wrong. You see while you were sleeping off the ketamine I used a palm scanner to encode your fingerprints so I could use them. The gloves Brooke wore when she shot Richard were laced with fibers that left your fingerprints on everything she touched. It's new tech BluTrend has been developing. In a few hours you'll no longer be declared a missing person, but a wanted one."

"The Hub's recordings will show I was nowhere near Richard when you killed him," I sneer.

"Not when I know how to manipulate their database… with help from your father."

"What did you do?" I ask, hitting him.

Pinning me to the bed, he shoves my arm down along my side as the other is still attached to the ring in the wall. "Nothing he wasn't more than willing to do for me at the right price."

"He'd never do anything to hurt me."

"Of course he wouldn't, but that's not what I told him. He knows you're missing and is desperate to find you. I simply promised to help in the search efforts if he told me how to access the Hub's network and navigate through their records without being noticed. I convinced him it was the easiest way to locate you and the stupid drunk fell for it."

Tears stream down my face. "He doesn't know anything."

"How long have you been telling yourself that lie?" Kane wipes them away.

"It's not a lie." I begin to choke on buried emotions quickly rising to the surface.

"You've known since the moment your mother's body was found that he killed her. CSB even has the evidence to convict him, but without you telling them the truth of what you know that'll never happen."

176

"It's not true," I utter, while I continue to sob. "My father loved my mother."

"Until she got pregnant with Richard's bastard child, then everything in his perfect little world fell apart."

"You know nothing about my family," I hiss.

"I know more than you do. I've spent hours going over her case, stealing information where I could, watching Detective Corro's interviews with Michael and the rage he displayed every time her affairs were brought up. I did my research on every bit of your life when I decided to make you mine. I left nothing unturned, no matter how painful or embarrassing. It's what helped create this entire plan."

"Frank is going to see right through your bullshit," I utter.

"Not when the chief backs the evidence they'll find against you. Frank won't have any choice but to go along with the rest of the bureau, or he'll have to find himself a new line of work."

"I don't believe you."

Kane searches the floor on my side of the bed, picks up the remote, and turns on the television. He scrolls through the various channels until one displaying my picture comes across the screen. He turns up the volume to make sure I can hear the reporter accurately.

"What started out as a missing persons case has now turned into a manhunt," a young woman says, coming into focus as my photo slides off to the side. "Detective Olivia Darrow has been missing since Monday afternoon, but as of this morning we've learned she may be responsible for the death of prominent technology mogul, Richard Cassidy. His body was found this morning near Foxtail Park, a gun range in Gardens which Detective Darrow is known to visit. Her weapon was found at the scene, which is also her last known location according to the Hub. We now go live to CSB headquarters where Chief William Daven is expected to make a statement."

The scene changes to one of the entrances into headquarters where a mob of reporters have gathered and a podium erected. Chief Daven looks grim, his dark features made even darker by his obvious foul mood. He's dressed in a suit, which is normal, while his mouth is clenched tight as a vein bulges in his neck. Several CSB officers stand behind him, but I don't see Frank, or even Gabe, among them.

"It's a terrible day when one of our own takes a life, but it's made even more painful when it's done for revenge," Chief Daven says, his deep voice booming. "Olivia Darrow was a highly decorated homicide detective and beloved by all her colleagues. She's lived through personal tragedy, which may have precipitated in the death of Richard Cassidy. Nancy Darrow, Olivia's mother, was murdered over twenty years ago and the case has never been solved. It has been brought to CSB's attention that Detective Darrow may have come across information regarding her mother's case in which it was revealed that she and Richard Cassidy had an affair. It is our belief that Detective Darrow used this knowledge to lure Mr. Cassidy away from his estate on Waterside with the intention of murdering him as she felt he was the cause of her mother's death and the destruction of her family. Even though a gun was located at the scene, Detective Darrow is considered armed and extremely dangerous. Anyone who sees her is to contact the nearest CSB station."

"You see," Kane turns off the television, "the only safe place for you to be is here with me."

"You're a fucking idiot," I retort. "Frank isn't the only detective who'll be out looking for me."

"You're referring to Gail Rodgers. It's true she might find the connection between us and the women who went missing, but without any evidence to show who took them or where they went I'm not worried. If she comes knocking on the door I'm ready."

"You're over confident."

"And you keep underestimating me," he grouses. "Mabel will be babysitting you today as I have business matters to attend to now that Richard is gone. Behave yourself, or you'll find another needle with ketamine in your arm."

Kane kisses me, then leaves. It feels like hours before Mabel comes down, a gun clutched in her hand. She tosses me the keys to the handcuffs and I free myself, following her upstairs and into Kane's bathroom where I'm made to shower and put on clean clothes. She feeds me before taking me back down to my room where the door is locked, but I'm left to roam free. I take the time to look under the bed as I wasn't able to do that before. I squeeze myself under the frame hoping to loosen one of the screws holding it together, but the frame is welded. I begin ripping the thin covering for the bedspring hoping to free one. Slim wires are wrapped tightly around each spring, so I begin to unwind one as best as I can. My arms and fingers eventually grow tired, forcing me to stop.

This is my life for the next week. During the days I'm permitted upstairs with Mabel to eat and use the facilities, while during the night Kane retires to my room where I'm made to watch the evening news and the updates on the manhunt for me. He seems to be relishing his victory, but I know better. No one can be fooled that easily. Something always falls through, an unexpected snare appears, or people are underestimated. This will all fail for Kane. It's just a matter of time.

I hardly see Brooke when I'm out of my cell. When I do, she glowers at me with such hatred it fills the entire room. I'm sure she wishes Kane would kill me like their father wanted, but he's adamant to keep me no matter my protests, which have started to wind down the more I languish in my room without any end in sight. I know none of my friends or coworkers believe the crap being broadcasted by the media, yet no one has come out to contradict their claims. Not even Joe.

After dinner, Mabel escorts me down and locks me away. I crawl under the mattress to continue working on the springs I've gotten to loosen, freeing one of them. As I sit on the bed, unwinding one end from another wire holding it curled into place the television turns on. I'm half expecting to see something from around the house that Kane wants me to watch, only the video that begins to play isn't anything I'm expecting.

Kane's bedroom comes into view along with a slightly younger version of himself, perhaps five years younger. His moans and grunts are all too familiar to me as he beds a young woman, her howls of delight matching his.

"Tell me again, Kane," the young woman begs as her voice registers in my mind even though I can't see her face.

"Once this is all over it'll just be you and me," he utters. "No one will get between us ever again."

"What if Richard finds out?"

"I'll take care of him when the time is right, Brooke," Kane says before letting out a howl as he comes. "It'll just be the two of us, I promise."

The video changes to one of Brooke's room with the two of them in her bed. This time she's in full view of the camera as Kane fucks her from behind. The cycle continues for what I can only assume are years as they both grow slightly older with time. I become more and more sickened with each display and wish it would stop. Kane repeats many times to Brooke that it'll just be the two of them as soon as their scheme is complete. She squeals with delight as he fucks her relentlessly.

The door to the hallway outside of my room squeaks when it opens. I stash the spring under my pillow just as the television shuts off. Kane enters after unlocking the door, a devilish smile creasing his face.

"I've been waiting all day to see you," he says, coming over to me.

"Don't touch me." I shove him away. "Don't come near me."

"What's the matter?" he asks, looking perplexed. "I thought we were starting to get along."

"There's no way in hell of that ever happening," I say, kicking him in the chest, causing me to fall off the bed and onto the floor as he crashes into the wall by the door. I hurry to my feet, but I don't get far when Kane grabs my hair, pulling me back onto the bed.

"Bitch," he says, then punches me. "If you thought things were bad before, I have new torments in store for you."

"Watching you fuck your sister was bad enough," I say as he straddles me, reaching for the handcuff that's still attached to the ring, slipping it around my wrist.

"What are you talking about?" he asks, raving.

180

"Go ask Brooke as I'm sure she's the one responsible for showing me the recordings the two of you made."

"When?"

"Just before you came down." I thrash about, trying to dislodge myself as my free hand fumbles to grab the spring. "I saw everything. If you thought there was any chance of turning me around, it's now gone forever. I hope CSB finds me as I'd rather be known as a murdered than your girlfriend."

He raises his fist to hit me again, but pauses midair.

"I'll be right back," he says, seething.

The minute the door closes I take the spring and begin prying bits of the drywall away from the plate, chiseling what I can and tugging when I begin to make headway. Shouting from above distracts me briefly, but I go back to work as we've reached the threshold I knew was coming and I have no time to listen to anything but my own heartbeat. I pull as hard as I can, cutting my wrist with the handcuff, but the anchor and plate begin to move. I use the spring to pry the screws loose and almost have it freed when shots ring out. I try not to think about it until the door to my room bursts open, Brooke stumbling in with a gun pointed at me.

"Your turn," she hisses.

Swinging my leg, my foot catches her arm, causing the gun to fly out of her hand. As she drops to retrieve it, I pull as hard as I can on the ring, the anchor finally giving way, releasing the metal plate from the wall. I swing it at Brooke when she rises with the weapon, and the corner of the plate hits her in the eye. She screams as blood spurts from the deep wound, but I don't wait around to see what the injury looks like. I scramble to my feet and am running out of the doorway when a shot fires, a searing pain radiating along my side. Falling against the wall, blood cascades down my leg from a wound just above my left hip. I stumble toward the stairs and out into the study, leaving a trail as I go.

Lightning flashes and thunder rolls outside while I make my way through the house. When I reach the foyer, I find Mabel lying face down, her body against the front door, blood pooling around her. I try to shove her away, but she's too heavy. I glance around for Kane, not seeing him anywhere, which only adds to my growing anxiety. I hear Brooke barreling up the staircase, so I make a decision to head toward the family room since that has the closest exit. My feet slide under me, my blood continuing to fall, making the floor slippery. I manage to get the exterior door open, rain pelting me when another shot rings out, this one penetrating my right shoulder blade. I scream as the bone shatters, but I keep pushing on, though I don't make it far.

I collapse onto my knees on the brick around the pool. My lungs burn, pain radiating through my body. I'm knocked to the ground and rolled onto my back, which only makes things worse. Brooke straddles me, pressing the barrel of the gun against my forehead, burning my skin. I cry out at the agony she's causing by adding pressure to my initial wound.

"Why did you have to come into our lives?" Brooke mutters while the rain soaks us.

Noticing the metal plate sliced through part of her eye, almost dislodging the organ, I try not to gag at the sight.

"Drop the gun," Kane demands, standing beside me, his own weapon aimed at Brooke's head.

Between the flashes of lightning I notice a deep cut along his temple, blood seeping out and mixing with the rain like my own.

"This is all her fault," Brooke growls. "It was supposed to be just the two of us when this was all over and done with. She ruined everything!"

"I know, Brooke," Kane says as calmly as possible. "You need to let me handle it."

"I tried, but you couldn't let her go. You left me no choice, Kane. I had to show her our movies and the promises you made to me. She had to know the truth before she died."

"And you were right in showing her. I was wrong to have cast you aside like I did. Let me punish Olivia for the mistake." Kane uses his free hand to caress Brooke's cheek. "I can make this all go away if you just give me the gun."

Brooke looks up, sorrow in her eyes as Kane lowers his weapon.

Smiling, she stands, and places the gun into his hand. "I love you, Kane."

"I know," he replies, then fires several shots directly into her chest.

She falls backward into the pool, sinking below its surface as Kane drops the weapons onto the ground and begins tending to my wounds.

"I knew she was crazy." Pressing his hand against my side, he tries to stem the bleeding. "I should never have allowed it to get this far. I should've killed her the same night she murdered Richard. God damn it. I can't get this to stop. I'm calling for an ambulance."

As he reaches into his back pocket for his cell phone a thick pair of hands wrap around his throat, pulling him away.

"Olivia!" Kane screams while he's dragged away by several CSB officers. They pin him to the ground. "Get off me!"

"Liv," Frank cries, his horrified face coming into view, noticing my wounds. "I need a medic!"

"Tell Dean I'm sorry," I utter, everything growing darker.

"Liv, don't you dare quit on me," Frank demands. "Where's that God damn medic?!"

"I can't." My hearing begins to wane and cold infiltrates my soul. "Tell Dean I'm sorry."

"Olivia!" Kane hollers, his voice fading into the night along with the rest of the world.

Twelve

My body feels heavy, like it's been weighted down. An incessant beep penetrates my brain, gnawing at my nerves with each passing second. Slowly opening my eyelids, I notice I'm in a hospital room filled with vases of flowers, lying covered in warm blankets. I turn my head and realize the beeping is coming from a machine my body is hooked up to, monitoring my heartrate. It takes a few seconds for me to realize my right arm is in an immobilizer to keep it still while my left is attached to an IV drip with a pouch of morphine attached to the bag. I go to move my right hand, but it proves difficult and I'm hoping it's because of the narcotics. Feeling someone holding onto my left, I look down and spot Dean's head resting on top of the bed, his eyes closed as he snores quietly.

"He hasn't left your side since you were brought in," Frank says, entering.

"How long have I been here?"

"Only a few days. I've had to force him to leave a few times to shower and eat. He doesn't like leaving you alone, so if he's not here Joe or I fill in. It was the only way we could get him to take a break."

"I'm surprised he's even talking to me," I utter, my voice weak. "Where am I?"

"Grove Hospital. The chief had you transferred here once you were stable. He didn't want you staying at the hospital on Waterside considering you're accused of killing a prominent member of their society."

"I didn't kill Richard Cassidy," I say, trying to sound furious as my heartrate increases.

"Settle down, Liv," Frank says, coming over to me. "I know you didn't, and soon so will everyone else. We knew the minute Richard's body was found that you weren't involved. It was at that point Gabe, Gail, and I began monitoring the estate. We heard gunshots and were in the midst of breaching the front door when Kane shot Brooke."

"Where's Kane?"

"He's being held in isolation at the detention facility. The prosecutor made a deal. He won't pursue the death penalty if Kane confesses to murdering those five missing women."

"And?"

"Kane took the deal despite what his lawyer tried to say. He wanted a trial to prove Kane doesn't have a sound mind, therefore he isn't responsible for his actions. He'll be moved to solitary confinement in the prison tomorrow." Frank pauses, and I can tell there's more on his mind. "He's asking to see you."

"Hell no," I almost shout, which disturbs Dean.

"Babe, you're awake," he says, smiling. "I was so worried."

"Robert, can you give us a minute?"

Dean scowls at the name. "I'll be in the hall," he says, then leaves.

Frank sits in the vacated chair looking troubled.

"What is it?" I ask, growing annoyed by the silence.

"It's your father," he replies, his face falling. "When he learned how Kane used him to access the Hub's computers, he couldn't handle the guilt of helping a madman set you up for murder. Randy found him yesterday hanging from the rod in his closet."

I turn my head away as knots form in my stomach and my heart shatters. Tears force their way to the surface, but I don't want to shed them for a man who abandoned me years ago.

"He left a note," Frank continues. "It's more of a confession than anything."

"I don't want to know," I whimper.

"Bev wants to see you. I'll let her know you're awake," he says, then leaves.

Dean returns, retaking his chair and his hold on my hand, but I can't look at him. I feel overwhelmed and alone.

"Why did he have to tell me now?" I utter.

"There's never a right time for news like that," Dean says. "Frank knew you needed to hear it before someone else told you."

185

"He was a selfish bastard until the very end. When can I get out of here?"

"Not for at least another couple of days. Then I'll take you home."

"Are you going to stay with me?"

"I don't know," he replies, his demeanor souring. "You really hurt me, Liv. I never thought you capable of cheating."

"We weren't a couple," I say. "According to you we were simply fuck buddies. You don't say something like that if you want to be in a relationship with someone."

"But you continued to sleep with Kane even after I made it clear my feelings for you," he says, his ire rising.

"I felt backed into a corner, Dean. You were making all these decisions regardless of what I wanted. I told you I don't do relationships."

"And now you don't have any," he says, abruptly standing, storming out of the room.

I slump down in the bed as best I can, but it's difficult. I've fucked up everything and now I'm truly alone.

"What's the matter with Robert?" Frank asks, returning.

"Nothing," I grumble.

"Bev is on her way. Do you want me to stay with you until she arrives?"

"I don't care. Do whatever you want."

He sits beside me and doesn't say a word.

"How did you discover I was missing?" I ask after a lengthy silence.

"Dean went to your house to pick up his things. He knew immediately something was wrong when he saw the Nimbus parked on the back driveway, the alarm was off, your purse was inside the house, and he spotted drops of blood on your carpet. He called me in hysterics believing your dad had gotten into the house, but I had other suspicions."

"Why?"

"Because of your call to Gail advising her to run a DNA test on the missing women against Brooke Cassidy. I spoke with Joe since he's a close friend of the family. He told me about you and Kane, going into great detail about the party the night after the fight."

"Was Dean ever a suspect?"

"No," Frank answers, rubbing the back of his neck as if uncomfortable. "I knew he didn't have anything to do with it by his reaction to you missing. The guy was a wreck. I instructed Luke to keep him at the arena so he wouldn't interfere with the investigation. When Gabe and I went to the estate to speak with Kane and he slipped up about your car not being parked in the driveway. I knew it was him, I just couldn't prove it at the time."

"I saw you. Kane has cameras all over the estate. The room I was being held in had a television and he made me watch the encounter."

"We found it when we searched the house."

"What's going to happen to BluTrend?"

"They have a board of directors that will clean up the mess Kane created. CSB has seized their chip modifying technology and they've been barred from producing anything new along those lines. The government will be auditing their offices and warehouses for the next several years to ensure they remain in compliance. It's the same with Centurion. Anything under that shell company's name will now be handled by BluTrend. I wouldn't be surprised if they sell it."

"I'm going to need a new microchip."

"No, you won't. Hayden's team found the kill code Kane used to disarm the chip, so yours has been reactivated."

"How did he manage to do that?"

"By using one from the missing women. The microchips record everything no matter how minimal. You just need to know where to look. Also, with the information your father left behind the Hub has been able to close off the security loopholes that allowed Kane access to the system."

"I guess I need to start thinking about making arrangements."

"Joe and I are handling that. Rudy is going to need his apartment cleaned out eventually, but that can be done whenever you're ready."

"He can throw it all out. I don't want anything from that man."

"You don't have to decide that now," Frank says, patting my hand as there's a knock on the door.

"Am I interrupting?" Bev inquires, lingering in the doorway.

"No, I was just leaving." Frank gets to his feet. "I'll be back later."

Bev takes his seat as Frank closes the door behind him.

"I really don't want to do this now."

"I'm here as a friend, Olivia. Not your therapist."

I want to try and keep my emotions bottled up like I have been since I woke, but having Bev here makes that nearly impossible.

"I've fucked everything up," I cry, tears raining down my face. "My life has been destroyed because I refused to accept responsibility for my actions."

"Are you talking about what happened with Dean or Kane?"

"Both."

"Kane was out of your control, Olivia. He was never going to take no for an answer and could've possibly made your life much worse. Once he set his sights on you he would've done anything to obtain you, and I mean *anything*, regardless of the consequences to him or you. You could've easily wound up with his other trophies in that rose garden. He has the type of personality where he needs to be in control of everything and everyone. I won't be surprised if they manage to add more missing women to his list, even if they weren't sired by his father."

"Dean's gone," I say, my heart hurting even more than it already does as I begrudgingly admit the loss. "I finally managed to chase him away right at the time I need him the most."

"You knew that could happen with the choices you were making."

"How do I fix this?"

"I honestly don't know if it can be. You may have to move on and put this behind you."

"That's going to be difficult considering I won't be permitted back to work with a busted arm."

"After a few months of therapy I'm sure Frank can put you on light duty work until you pass the physical to be reinstated. You haven't said anything about your father."

"Do I have to?" I grouse.

"No, but part of moving on is dealing with the hurt and betrayal he caused you."

"I thought you were here as a friend."

"I am. Sometimes the therapist in me just comes out." She pauses for a brief moment before continuing. "Did you suspect he killed your mother?"

"Maybe on some level I did," I reply. "But I could never figure out why until recently."

"Do you want to read his letter?"

"No," I answer quickly. "Look, Bev, I'm tired."

"I'll let you rest," she says, patting my leg as she stands, then leaves.

My head hurts from crying, but I continue to do so until I fall asleep.

I'm finally discharged three days later. Joe is driving me home. He says the girls miss me and send their love. Frank and Gail made sure to stock my cupboards so I wouldn't have to run out for anything. If I do need something, I'm to call one of them as neither want me driving since my arm is still in the immobilizer for at least another week or two. The house has an unsettling feel when I step inside. Dean's absence is heavily felt as his boxes are gone along with everything he had in the bathroom and closet.

"Do you need me to help you with anything while I'm here?" Joe asks when I return to the living room.

"No. I'll be fine."

Joe hugs me gingerly before leaving, and I turn on the alarm once the door is closed. I wander over to the desk, noticing my purse is still where I left it when Riddle attacked me, but thankfully the horrid white box is gone. Making my way into the garage, I discover the Nimbus is parked in its usual spot and realize my things are still in the apartment above the club. I call Frank and tell him.

"Gail and I are heading over there now to collect the files. I'll make sure to grab everything."

"Leave behind the blankets, sheets, and towels," I instruct. "You never know when I might need to stay there again."

Finding myself growing bored as the day stretches, I take a blanket and curl up on the couch to watch a movie. I get through several before Frank arrives. He turns off my alarm before carting my bags into the house, setting them down in the bedroom. Then, he takes off his jacket, laying it across the desk chair.

"I ordered a pizza for us, so it should be here soon," he says, sitting beside me while I gaze at the television, only half paying attention to it. "Your dad's burial is scheduled for tomorrow afternoon. Joe will be coming by around one to pick you up. We decided on a simple service at the gravesite. He's being buried next to your mother." His concerned stare continues to linger. "Have you heard from Dean?"

"No, and I don't expect to," I reply, a lump catching in my throat at the thought of him.

"When do you start physical and occupational therapy?"

"Next week. Nikki from the club is going to take me. Joe's paying her to do it."

"Have they said how long that'll take?"

"Eight weeks minimum, and I'll be going twice a week."

"I can't let you back to work until you complete your recertification test."

"I know."

"Randy and I had all of your father's things moved into a storage locker in Berrin in case you decide to rummage through it someday."

My doorbell rings, and the camera on my front porch displays a young man holding a cardboard box. Frank pays for the food, sets the box on the coffee table, then heads into the kitchen, coming back with napkins and beer. We barely speak while we eat, which I can tell is bothering him, but I'm too depressed to care. My thoughts are filled with Dean and how much I miss him. He's been a part of my life for so long I never realized how large of a void there would be if and when he left.

After thanking Frank for the food, I tell him to lock up the house and set the alarm when he leaves as I head off to bed though it's still early in the evening. I stay in the cotton shorts and shirt I currently have on, get under the covers, and cry myself to sleep as I have been for the last several days.

Showering is difficult since I have limited motion with my right arm and it kills to use it. I do the best I can, don a simple black dress, put the immobilizer back on, then grab something to eat as Joe will be arriving shortly. I carry very little with me as we pull out of the driveway and head toward the onramp for the highways that circle the sectors, allowing travel between the states. The cemeteries are several miles outside of the state proper in federally owned territory since there isn't any room in the states themselves. The one my mother is buried in is closest to Berrin, but it'll take us over an hour to reach. We wind down the many narrow lanes until we come to the section where my family plot is located.

Chairs have been erected on the grass while a silver coffin rests on top of a lowering device that will nestle my father's remains into the ground. A large bouquet of flowers sits beside the coffin, and I notice Frank speaking with a man in a clergy outfit, though my family isn't religious. Joe assists me from the car while others begin to arrive, mainly those I work with at CSB in addition to Bev and a couple of the girls from the club. Frank introduces me to the priest after giving me the perfunctory hug and peck on the cheek, then I take a seat in the front row with him and Joe on either side of me. Once everyone else has seated the service begins, but I tune out

191

everything since I feel numb, flashing back on memories of when we had to do this for my mother. It comes to an end and I stand to place a lone flower on the casket, then everyone comes up to me, giving their condolences.

"Joe, can I have a few minutes alone with Olivia," Frank says.

"I'll wait for you at the car," he says, squeezing my hand.

"I brought your father's letter in case you changed your mind."

"Stop forcing it on me," I snap. "I don't give a damn what that bastard had to say. He murdered two women he claimed to love. There's nothing in that note that will change my opinion about him."

"He only confessed to killing your mother, not Lesley Marsh."

"It still doesn't mean he's not responsible."

"We cleared him as a suspect a few days ago," Frank says, looking a little sheepish. "After going through hours of drone footage for that night we discovered a man passed out in an alley around the time Lesley was presumed to have been killed. The cameras identified him as your father. We weren't able to find any recordings of Lesley, though, so the case is still open and we've run out of leads. Gabe will continue to work it, but I don't see him getting very far with the lack of evidence we have."

"It still doesn't change the fact that he took my mother away from me."

"No, sweetheart, it doesn't." Frank pulls me against his chest as I cry. "Let's head back to your house. Bev is going there to set up a brief buffet for everyone to enjoy."

"I want a few minutes alone."

Releasing me, he heads toward his vehicle, which is parked behind Joe's. Filled with mixed emotions, I stare down at the casket. I hate my father for what he did, but I understand the anger behind it. There had to have been more going on between them to cause him to snap, but I'll never know. A week ago life was simple, but now it's turned chaotic and unpredictable... and lonely. I want to scream as a way to vent my anger and frustration, except I can't find the power within myself to accomplish that. I'm broken, shattered beyond repair. I should've confronted him years ago, but then I'd have to face the fact that my life was a lie, maybe even a mistake neither of them could remedy. He should've murdered me as well that night, then I wouldn't be going through this heartache.

"Hi, Liv," Dean says, standing on the other side of the casket, his hands shoved into the pockets of his dress pants. He looks rugged and handsome in his suit, which only causes me more pain.

"What are you doing here?" I ask in a weakened voice.

"I came to see how you're doing."

"I'm taking it day by day. You?"

"I'm not going to lie, it's been rough."

"Give it time. The pain will pass. I should get going."

"Where are you headed?"

"My house. They're throwing a luncheon."

"Would you mind if I stopped by?"

"I'd like that," I say, smiling, which is something I haven't done in a while.

Joe opens the car door for me when I approach, then we head back to Range. Frank must have given Bev my alarm code as she's already inside of the house setting up when we arrive. Small sandwiches, a vegetable plate, and an assortment of cookies line my kitchen counters while a punch bowl sits filled almost to the brim on my dinette. Frank makes a plate for me while I sit in the living room. Most of the officers who weren't at the service due to work stop by to give their condolences, as does Gail and Gabe. The day passes in a blur with various people coming and going throughout the late afternoon and into the evening. I don't see Dean, which makes me even more miserable than I already am.

Bev and Frank work on cleaning up the mess while Joe hugs me goodnight as he leaves. Bev places the leftovers in my fridge, that way I don't have to cook for at least a couple of days. After thanking them both, I set the alarm as soon as they're out the door. I begin to head to the bedroom to undress when my doorbell chimes. Glancing at the screen by the door, I spot Dean standing nervously on the porch. I disarm the alarm and unlock the door.

"Sorry I wasn't here earlier," he says, stepping into the house. "I kind of wanted us to be alone."

"There's food in the fridge if you're hungry." I close the door and head into the kitchen. As I pass, Dean grabs my hand.

"I just want us to talk."

"Do you mind if I change first? You know how much I hate being in a dress all day."

He smiles and gestures toward the bedroom. Closing the door behind me, I remove the immobilizer so I can undress. My arm feels heavy when the device is off and I have to massage the muscles a little so they don't stiffen.

"Where did you get those scars?" Dean asks from the doorway, startling me.

"Riddle did this to me while he was holding me at Requiem until Kane came to collect me," I reply.

"Is that the only place he hurt you?"

"Yes, fortunately," I answer, then unzip my dress, stepping out of it as it lies on the floor so I can put on my cotton shorts and shirt.

"Your wing is broken," Dean says, moving behind me, his finger outlining the scar made by the entry wound from Brooke's bullet.

"It's befitting to my current state of mind. Perhaps I'll leave it so the whole world will know how damaged I am."

"You're not damaged. Tarnished maybe, but not damaged."

"Thanks, that makes me feel a whole lot better," I retort as I begin to dress.

"Frank showed me the pictures of the room where you were kept. Along with the cuff and anchor that had to be cut free from your wrist when you were brought to the hospital."

"Why the hell would he do that?"

"So I could understand what Kane put you through."

194

"When did he show you?"

"The day you were released from the hospital. He was furious when I told him I wasn't going to pick you up like I promised. That's why Joe was there instead of me."

"What does it matter?" I utter, my back still toward him as tears begin to fall. "Nothing can change the awful things I've done."

"I also spoke with Bev."

"Fuck, Dean, why?" I ask, turning to face him.

"She asked me to see her so she could explain to me what type of person Kane is and why he put you through that nightmare."

"So you're only here to take pity on me?" My voice cracks as the tears begin to flow heavier. "I don't need your empathy or condescension, Dean. I've been torturing myself well enough as it is. You can leave."

"Why do you always make things difficult?" he snaps. "I'm trying to offer my sympathy and you're throwing it back into my face."

"Fuck your sympathy," I rave. "I don't need it."

"Then what do you need?"

I go to open my mouth and admit the truth, but it terrifies me. I've lived in fear for days like this my entire life, but I'll never grow as a person if I don't let my vulnerability show at least a little.

"I need you," I finally reply. "It's been horrible since you left. I hate that you're not in bed beside me every night. I miss you harassing me to the point of fighting and the intense sex that always follows. I can't tolerate being in this house without you. I never realized how much I needed you until you were gone. I love you, God damn it."

He kisses me as he wraps me in his warm arms. We can't get our clothes off fast enough, which is made even more difficult by the injury to my arm. I arch my back as he slips inside, then he lifts me up and slams me onto the bed. My moans fill the air as Dean fucks me as hard as possible. I come several times before he does. He steps away from the bedroom for a brief moment to lock the door and set the alarm, then returns and we don't let each other go until morning.

Lightning Source UK Ltd.
Milton Keynes UK
UKHW020651310521
384676UK00011B/748